HALL of MIRRORS

A place for reflection

Don't CRACK Under the pressure

HorrorLand

www.EnterHorrorLand.com

THE STREETS OF PANIC PARK

R.L. STINE

SCHOLASTIC INC.
New York Toronto London Auckland
Sydney Mexico City New Delhi Hong Kong

No part of this publication may be reproduced, stored in a retrieval system, or transmitted in any form or by any means, electronic, mechanical, photocopying, recording, or otherwise, without written permission of the publisher. For information regarding permission, write to Scholastic Inc., Attention: Permissions Department, 557 Broadway, New York, NY 10012.

ISBN 978-0-439-91880-0

Goosebumps book series created by Parachute Press, Inc.

Goosebumps HorrorLand #12: *The Streets of Panic Park* copyright © 2009 by Scholastic Inc.

All rights reserved. Published by Scholastic Inc., *Publishers since 1920.* SCHOLASTIC, GOOSEBUMPS, GOOSEBUMPS HORRORLAND, and associated logos are trademarks and/or registered trademarks of Scholastic Inc.

12 11 10 9 8 7   11 12 13 14/0

Printed in the U.S.A.
First printing, July 2009

THE STORY SO FAR...

Captured. Sixteen kids.

Captured and taken to an enormous mansion. It looked like a castle with black stone walls and dark towers rising up on both sides.

I'm Lizzy Morris. I'm thirteen. My brother Luke is eleven.

Yes, we were too young to face the kind of horror we found at Panic Park.

We weren't prepared for that kind of evil. We didn't expect someone like the man dressed all in black who stood over us now.

How did it start?

Fourteen kids had been invited to HorrorLand Theme Park as Very Special Guests. They looked forward to a week of scary fun. But they soon discovered the scares were too REAL.

The kids knew they were in danger. They became desperate to escape HorrorLand and get to another park, a place called Panic Park. A HorrorLand worker — a Horror named

Byron — was their only friend. He told them they would be safe in Panic Park.

Luke and I had been to HorrorLand before. Someone at the park started sending us information online about the kids. He called himself Monster X. He told us that Panic Park was a *horrifying* place — that the kids would be safer in HorrorLand.

Luke and I hurried to the park to warn the kids.

When we arrived, eight kids had already escaped to Panic Park. Luke and I tried to tell the remaining kids what we had learned. We told them to stay in HorrorLand.

But the kids were frantic to follow their friends to the other park.

A girl named Jillian Gerard said she had the power to read minds. She stared into my eyes. She told the other kids I was lying. She said Luke and I were working with the Horrors to keep them in HorrorLand.

Byron helped the kids escape to Panic Park. They didn't want my brother and me to come with them. But we followed them anyway. We thought maybe we could help them.

Panic Park turned out to be a nightmare place. No color at all. The whole park was in black and white. Strange, sad shadow people followed us everywhere. We didn't see anyone else.

We found a newspaper that said Panic Park had closed in 1974.

Did we travel back in time? Were we in some kind of parallel universe?

We were totally confused.

We only knew for sure that Panic Park was *much* more terrifying than HorrorLand.

And now, here we were — all sixteen of us — in this gloomy, cold mansion.

We stared at the man in front of us. He stood on a stage behind a tall podium. He called himself The Menace.

Even before he spoke, even before he told us his name, we knew he was someone we should fear. . . .

1

The Menace was dressed in black from head to toe. His shirt and tie, his pants, his jacket, his shoes, were the deepest black. He wore black gloves. And his face was completely hidden in the shadow of a wide-brimmed black hat.

We had been forced to march down long, dark halls. The walls were gray. The plaster cracked and peeling. I saw no windows.

We ended up in a huge, empty chamber. Our footsteps scraped loudly over the stone floor.

The gray walls were bare. They rose up forever to a balcony that overlooked the chamber.

At the front of the room there was a stage. And a podium. And the man dressed in black. There were no chairs in front of the stage. We stood awkwardly, huddled together.

Behind us, the door was blocked by shadow people. They watched silently as The Menace gripped the podium with his gloved hands.

"Well, well, well...don't all of you look FRIGHTENED!" he said. His voice rang off the high stone walls.

Matt Daniels is tall and athletic. He is one of the bravest kids. He stepped forward and shouted up to the stage. "Why did you bring us here? What do you want?"

The Menace uttered a cold laugh. "Love the sound of your *fear*!" he cried. "LOVE it! LOVE it!"

Matt stepped back. He muttered something to Carly Beth Caldwell. Carly Beth is little and pixyish and looks much younger than her age — twelve.

Luke and I stood behind them. I couldn't hear what Matt said.

The Menace's words still rang in my ears. His voice was deep but hoarse at the same time.

His icy laugh raised the hairs on the back of my neck.

"How does it feel to be so completely AFRAID?" he asked. "Do you think it's possible to be *scared to death*? Well, good friends... we're going to test that out — aren't we!"

Luke squeezed my hand. "Is he for real?" he whispered.

I started to answer, but the words caught in my throat.

Billy Deep and his sister, Sheena, took a few steps back from the stage. They kept glancing behind us to the door. Probably thinking of making a run for it.

Britney Crosby and her friend Molly Molloy couldn't hide the fear from their faces. They stood with their arms crossed tightly in front of them and their jaws clenched.

"We escaped HorrorLand to come to this place!" Matt shouted up to the stage. "We were told we'd be safe here."

"Safe?" The Menace replied. "No one is safe in MY park!" He slapped the podium with both hands. "Uh-oh, guys. Don't look now, but I think someone LIED to you."

His words created an uproar. We all started talking at once.

And then Matt and Michael Munroe stepped in front of Jillian and her twin brother, Jackson. Matt balled his fists at his sides. "YOU'RE the ones who lied to us!" he cried.

We formed an angry circle around Jillian and Jackson.

"You *tricked* us into coming to Panic Park," Carly Beth said. "Lizzy told the truth — that we'd be safer in HorrorLand. But you told us she was lying."

"We thought you were our friends!" Carly Beth's friend Sabrina Mason said in a trembling voice. "How could you DO that to us?"

Michael is big and powerful. His nickname back home is Monster.

He pushed his face right up to Jillian's. "Admit it," he said angrily. "Admit it, Jillian. You tricked us into coming here — because you and your brother were working for The Menace the whole time!"

"NO!" Jillian cried. She stumbled back, trying to get away. But Michael stayed right in her face.

"It's not true!" Jackson shouted. "Leave my sister alone!"

"We ... we were never working for The Menace!" Jillian stuttered, her face bright red. "It's not true. It's not TRUE!"

"Oh, but it IS true!" the voice from the stage called.

I gasped. A silence fell over the big room.

"It *is* true!" The Menace said to the twins. "Don't lie to your friends."

"But ... but ..." Jillian stammered.

The Menace raised a gloved hand to silence her. "Where do you think your special powers came from? From that tacky wooden fortune-teller? Of *course* not. Your powers came *special delivery* from yours truly, the one and only Menace!"

"No!" Jillian cried, shaking her head again and again. "No! No!"

"We didn't know!" Jackson exclaimed. He turned to Matt and Michael and the rest of us.

"We didn't *know* we were helping The Menace! I *swear!*"

"You're both liars!" Michael cried.

"No —" Jackson tried to duck away.

But Michael punched him hard in the stomach, then tackled him to the stone floor. Grunting and groaning, the two boys wrestled at our feet.

"Stop it! STOP it!" Jillian screamed, her hands pressed tightly to her cheeks.

"Love it! LOVE it!" called The Menace, thumping the podium with his gloved fists. "I can SMELL the fear in this room!"

Michael gave Jackson one last punch, then he jumped up.

Jackson lay sprawled on his back, groaning and rubbing his sore stomach.

"Oh, come on." The Menace sighed. "Don't you want to fight some more? You *know* it makes me happy."

I squinted hard, trying to see the face under the wide brim of the black hat. But I could see only shadow.

Is there a face under there?

The Menace raised one arm and waved to the shadow people at the back of the chamber. "Come over here, shades. Take Jillian and Jackson away."

"Huh?" Jillian let out a cry.

"Take them away," The Menace ordered.

"They've done their job brilliantly. But . . . I have no more use for them."

"Wait —" Jackson cried. "What do you MEAN?"

"What are you going to *do* to us?" Jillian wailed.

But they didn't get an answer.

Shadow people slid around them. Covered them in a blanket of darkness. And herded them out of the room through a narrow door behind the stage.

I shuddered. I could still hear the twins screaming from the other side of the door.

The Menace leaned over the podium toward us. "How frightening is *that*?" he said. "Ooh, I'm shaking. I'm tingling all over. And the fun hasn't even started yet!"

I heard a noise. I turned in time to see Billy Deep spin around and break for the door behind us, his shoes clattering on the hard floor.

"Let's go! We're OUTTA here!" he screamed.

Sheena started to follow him.

"No — WAIT!" I cried. "Billy — DON'T!"

I saw the danger. I guess Billy didn't care.

He was almost to the entrance when a group of shadow people floated in front of him.

They wrapped themselves around him. For a long moment, we couldn't see him. He disappeared behind the shadows.

I held my breath. And watched him come bursting out — right through the shadow people.

We all saw him. We all saw what had happened to him.

But his sister, Sheena, was the first to scream. "NOOOO! Oh, NO! What have you done to my brother?"

Billy stopped and spun back to us.

I screamed. I couldn't help it. We were all screaming and crying out in shock.

The shadow people floated back to the doorway.

And Billy stood there, breathing hard, arms out at his sides.

Billy's face was gray, the color of ashes. His arms... his hands... all shadow. His body shimmered like smoke.

I couldn't see his eyes, his nose, his mouth. They were all a dark smudge! A shadow. Billy was only a shadow.

"What have you *done* to him?" Sheena wailed, running up to Billy. "Billy — are you okay? Can you see? Are you in there?"

Billy made a gulping sound. He glanced around, confused. I don't think he understood what had happened to him.

Finally, he raised his hands and stared at them. "I . . . I'm a shadow," he stammered. "So cold . . . Help me, Sheena. I feel so cold and strange."

"Too bad," The Menace called from the stage. He tsk-tsked. "Too bad, guys. Hard cheese, huh? Tough bananas. Billy Boy looked so much *cuter* before . . . when you could see his pretty face."

"Change him back!" Sheena screamed. "Change my brother back!"

Luke and I screamed, too. "Change him back! Change him back!" We all started yelling.

The Menace raised both hands to silence us. "Okay. No problem," he said. "First chance I get. I'll make a note to remind myself."

He laughed, an icy laugh that sent chills down my neck.

Billy moaned. "But . . . I'm not ME! I feel so light . . . like smoke that could blow away."

"Very nicely said," The Menace told him. "You should be a poet, Billy Boy. But let me give you one bit of advice. Next time you tangle with my devoted shadow people, at least make a fight of it. I need to see more fighting. I really do."

"He's totally nuts!" Luke whispered in my ear.

"And evil," I added. "Does he think his jokes are funny?"

13

"I don't think he cares," Luke whispered. Then he shuddered. "Poor Billy . . ."

Michael tried to thump Billy's gray shoulder, but his hand went right through him. He took a deep breath. "Don't worry," he said. "We'll get you back to normal."

He turned to The Menace. "Let us go!" he shouted. "You can't keep us here against our will!"

"Of *course* I can," The Menace replied, leaning on his podium. "I can do whatever I want."

"We want to go home — now!" Carly Beth spoke up.

The Menace snickered. "Do you have *any idea* how far away from home you are? Time to catch on, people. You're not as dim as you look — are you? I'm The Menace. I can keep you here forever."

He pulled his hat lower on his head. "I can do anything I want," he repeated, "because this whole world is MINE!"

The shadow people at the door cheered. It sounded more like moaning than cheering.

The Menace bowed his head to them. "Thank you. At least my people know their job. To cheer my every word and move!"

"Why did you bring us here? What do you want?" Carly Beth demanded.

"It's simple, guys," The Menace said. "I need to *terrify* you."

14

"Why?" I cried. My voice shook. "Why do you need to terrify us?"

"You'll find out soon enough," he replied. "I need to make you scream till your throats are on fire." He leaned toward us. "Any problem with that?"

I stared up at him in dazed silence.

We had already sampled some of the scares of Panic Park. Did he really plan to torture us with more terrors?

What kind of horrifying trap had we walked into?

Matt stepped closer to the stage. "We've all dealt with evil before," he told The Menace. "Everyone here has faced powerful villains — and we defeated them."

"That's the truth," Michael said. He bumped knuckles with Matt. Then he turned to The Menace. "You think you're so scary because you dress in black and talk tough? Well, look at us. There are sixteen of us — and we're not scared of you."

The Menace pretended to tremble in fear. "Ooh, look. I'm shaking. I'm shaking."

Behind us, the shadow people all laughed — moaning, lifeless laughter.

16

The Menace rubbed his gloved hands together. "Very brave speech, Michael, my lad. But do you really think you've faced evil before? I don't think so. You have *no idea* what true terror is."

He thumped the podium with both hands. "I've had years and years to study evil," he said. "Years and years to create total fear."

He paused for a moment. Then he said softly, "Maybe you need a sample. A little proof."

A cold shiver ran down my spine.

The Menace waved to a shadow at the door. "Go to the holding chamber," he ordered. "Bring in my newest trophy."

The shade nodded its faceless, gray head and floated forward slowly. He was almost to the stage when The Menace stopped him.

"Hold it right there," The Menace said quietly. "You're too slow, mister. You should move quicker when I tell you to do something. That's why I keep *this* handy."

The Menace reached behind the podium and lifted a black hose. It looked like a vacuum cleaner hose. He raised the nozzle and pointed it at the shadow. He pushed a button, and I heard a whining roar.

"No — please!" the shadow cried. "Please — I'm *begging* you!"

The Menace tossed back his head. His laughter rose above the roar of the vacuum.

The shade raised his hands to protect himself.

17

He struggled to pull back. But the vacuum was too powerful.

I uttered a cry as his head disappeared, sucked into the roaring hose. His shoulders folded in like tissue paper — and vanished with a *thwupppp* into the vacuum nozzle.

Then his arms, his chest . . . his whole body.

I didn't want to watch. But I couldn't turn away. I stared, frozen in horror, until his feet were sucked into the hose. And he was gone.

Silence.

The Menace waved to another shade. This one didn't need to be told. He *flew* past the stage and disappeared through the doorway in the back wall.

My heart was racing. I felt dizzy.

The Menace had destroyed that shadow person so easily. He laughed while he did it.

He's powerful and deadly, I thought. *And totally crazy.*

What did he want with us? Did he just want to scare us to death — for *fun*? To amuse himself?

The Menace turned to the doorway. "Bring it!" he shouted. "Bring in my new trophy!"

The shadow appeared in the doorway.

I squinted to see what he was carrying. But it was too dark.

He floated toward us into the light. He raised the trophy high.

And I opened my mouth in a high shriek of horror.

He was holding JILLIAN'S HEAD!

I covered my eyes with a trembling hand.

I could hear other kids screaming. I heard sobs and cries of disbelief.

Even with my eyes covered, I still saw Jillian's head with its brown hair flowing behind it. The dark, wide-open eyes . . . the mouth drooping open.

"No . . . no . . . no . . . no . . ." Carly Beth moaned by my side.

I opened my eyes. I saw Sabrina bent over, puking on the floor. Abby and Julie were hugging each other tightly, tears pouring down their faces.

"I *thought* this trophy might get your attention!" The Menace said. "It's a beauty, isn't it? All that lovely brown hair."

He took Jillian's head from the shadow person. He gazed at it for a long moment.

"See?" he said, turning back to us. "I can do anything I want. ANYTHING!"

Luke huddled close to me. He kept swallowing hard, trying not to puke.

The Menace raised Jillian's head by her hair. "THINK FAST!" he shouted.

And he HEAVED the head at us!

I screamed. Luke ducked.

Robby Schwartz caught the head. He uttered a cry and staggered back. His eyes bulged with horror.

And then his expression changed as he got a closer look. "Hey!" he said. "Hey — it's *rubber*! It's not real!"

Kids gasped in surprise. I let out a long sigh of relief. "Only rubber?"

The Menace laughed. "April Fools, guys. Next time it WILL be real," he said. "Maybe it'll be YOUR ugly head!"

Luke wrapped his arm around my waist. His whole body was trembling.

"Why are you doing this?" I shouted to The Menace. "Why don't you let us go home?"

"Lizzy, where are your listening skills?" he asked. "I told you — I need to keep you here. I need you to survive the most terrifying horrors I can dream up. I need to collect your fear!"

He motioned to the shadow people guarding the entrance to the room.

They floated forward like a fog rolling in.

The air grew icy as they surrounded us. I began to shiver from the cold.

A shade clapped a silvery bracelet on my wrist and snapped it shut. The bracelet pressed tightly into my skin.

"Wh-what is this?" I stammered.

I heard the metallic snap of bracelets. Everyone was getting one.

"Don't panic, people," The Menace said. "At least, don't panic YET!"

He laughed at his own joke, and the shadow people joined in, chuckling softly.

"The bracelets measure your fear," The Menace said. "And when you feel fear, they will start to heat up and tingle. Oh, boy. So sweet! I can almost feel them tingling right now!"

Matt tugged hard at his bracelet, struggling to pull it off his wrist.

"I don't think you should try to pull the bracelets off," The Menace said. "You see, any hard tug — and they will *burn* themselves into your flesh."

The Menace leaned forward over the podium. "Go ahead," he said to Matt. "Give it a try. I love the smell of barbecue — don't you?"

With a scowl, Matt let go of the bracelet. He balled his hands into fists but kept them down at his sides.

"That's better," The Menace said. "Let's get the show on the road, shall we, people?"

My whole body trembled as I gazed down the row of kids. Everyone looked pale and shaken.

Robby still held the rubber Jillian head tight in his hands. Carly Beth hugged Sabrina. Boone Dixon had his eyes shut.

The Menace turned to the door behind him. "Bring out the Fear Meter!" he shouted.

I heard the rumble of something heavy. Like furniture being moved.

The rumble grew louder as someone wheeled the Fear Meter into the room. It looked like a grandfather clock, tall and narrow.

The Meter was wheeled in front of the stage. And then the worker pushing it stepped out from behind it.

And everyone let out a startled gasp. We stared at his purple fur, the yellow horns poking up from his head.

BYRON!

Byron stepped back from the Fear Meter and nodded at The Menace. He stared at us as he adjusted the straps on his overalls.

"Why did you trick us?" Robby yelled at the tall Horror.

"We thought you were helping us!" Carly Beth shouted. "We thought you were on our side!"

"You thought wrong," Byron replied.

"Are you all totally *clueless*?" The Menace said. "Did you really think Byron was your friend?"

"He lied to us like Jillian and Jackson did," Robby scowled. He tossed the rubber head at Byron. It bounced off the Horror's big chest and landed on the floor.

Everyone started talking at once. Luke turned to me. "They really thought Byron was their friend."

"He tricked them," I said. "Now we're ALL caught in his trap."

"People, people, get a grip!" The Menace waved his hands to get us quiet. "You aren't the only ones Byron fooled. He fooled all the Horrors at HorrorLand, too. They thought he was working with them to protect you. But he was *my guy* right from the start."

Matt shook his head. "I trusted you, Byron," he muttered. "You gave me that Panic Park key card. I thought you were trying to help us."

"That key card got you interested in Panic Park," Byron said. "That started you on your way here."

"You should feel flattered. My friend Byron is the one who chose you all," The Menace announced.

"Why?" Matt demanded. "Why *us*?"

Byron crossed his furry purple arms in front of his chest. "I chose you because you all proved you were brave when you defeated those villains back home," he said. "You NEED to be brave to survive what The Menace has waiting for you."

"We tried the Fear Meter with other kids," The Menace said. "And . . . well . . . why go into the messy details? Let's just say it *wasn't pretty!*"

"Why do you need us to be brave?" Matt demanded.

"What are you going to do with us?" I cried.

"Why do you want to frighten us?" Sabrina asked in a tiny voice.

The Menace thumped his gloved hands on the podium. "Good questions, gang," he said. "Keep thinking. Try to think of the most frightening moment of your lives. That will be a start."

Then he leaned over the podium, his face still hidden in shadow. "You brighter ones may have noticed that this park is stuck in 1974," he said. "There was great fear in the park then. So much fear, it spun us into another reality. It stuck us in time."

Luke grabbed my hand. "Is he serious?" he whispered.

"*Your* fear will bring us back," The Menace continued. "The energy from your fear will return Panic Park to its place in the real world."

"I . . . I don't understand," I stammered. "How long are you going to keep us here?" I asked.

"For as long as it takes," The Menace replied. He turned to the Fear Meter. "I tried other kids," he said. "But they weren't brave enough to survive the terror. Byron says you have proven your bravery. We'll see."

A grin spread over Byron's face. "Be afraid," he said. "Be very afraid!"

Without warning, The Menace grabbed the brim of his hat — and lifted it off his head.

My breath caught in my throat. I stared at his face, seeing it for the first time.

Cold, dark eyes, ringed with black circles. A

pencil-thin mustache beneath his pointed nose. Deep lines down his cheeks. A cold sneer on his lips.

"How do you plan to frighten us?" Matt cried. *"Tell us!"*

"Hey, buddy boy — YOU don't ask the questions around here!" The Menace boomed. "I do."

"NO — I do!" a loud, shrill voice cried. *"I ask the questions!"*

The Menace's head spun around —

— and I screamed.

We all screamed.

The Menace had ANOTHER FACE on the back of his head!

My scream echoed off the high walls.

I couldn't take much more of this. I turned to run. But the shadow people were at the door, blocking any escape.

When our screams died down, The Menace's other face spoke up. "Keep it up! What a *delicious* sound! Yes! Yes! I love those screams of horror! Love them to death!"

This face had a high, nasal voice. And glowing red skin, as if it were *burning*, on fire! The eyes were wild, big, and rolling crazily. Beneath its flaring bulb of a nose, I saw full lips over crooked teeth.

The Menace had a dark face — and a face the color of *flames*!

"Love it! Love it! Keep screaming!" the red face cried.

And then The Menace turned around again, and the first face spoke up in its low, deep voice: "As you can see, I'm not timid. I will do *anything*. I have nothing to lose — and everything to gain."

"Stop bragging! They get the idea!" the second face snapped.

"I'm not bragging," the first face insisted. "I'm telling them what they need to know." He raised two gloved fingers. "As you can see, I have you kids outnumbered two to one."

"And two heads are better than one!" the red face declared.

"You guys are going to bring my park back to the real world," the dark face said. "By the power of your terrified screams."

He turned to Byron, standing by the tall wooden piece of furniture. "Start up the Fear Meter," he ordered.

Byron reached into the back of the box. I heard a click. Then the machine started to hum.

Byron turned it so we could see the narrow tube on the front. It looked a little like a thermometer.

The Fear Meter hummed for a while. The hum grew louder. And I saw a red line climb from the bottom.

Yes. It was *exactly* like a thermometer. It had numbers etched on the side, from 1 to 100.

We all watched in silence as the red line slid up . . . up . . . until it stopped at 20.

"Oh, no," The Menace groaned. "People, people — you must do much better than this.

You're just not trying, guys. Your fear has got to hit one hundred!"

His head spun around, and the red face spoke up: "I'll bet we can find something *juicy* to get that fear climbing!"

He waved a gloved hand. The shadow people began to move. They floated silently across the room. They surrounded us.

I could feel the icy cold rolling off them. I started to shiver.

I couldn't see. They floated over us like a black cloud.

I felt a cold force, a pressure like powerful wind, pushing me one way, then the other.

"Luke?" I called to my brother. My voice was muffled under the thick blanket of shadows. "Luke? Luke? Are you okay?"

No reply.

I felt sick. My stomach felt tight and heavy.

I kept picturing The Menace and his two faces. Two faces on one head!

How did he do that to himself? Was that part of his plan to frighten us?

Suddenly, the shadows lifted. Light poured over me. I stood with the other kids, shivering from the cold. Luke huddled beside me, his teeth chattering.

I raised my eyes to the stage. The red line on the Fear Meter had risen to 25.

If this is how frightened we feel at twenty-five, how will we survive fear that reaches fifty? Or one hundred?

I turned to The Menace. "Why won't you answer our questions?" I asked. "Why won't you tell us what you plan to do with us?"

His dark eyes peered down at me. "You will help me get Panic Park out of 1974," he said. "You will —"

His other face spun around. "Don't tell them!" he cried. "Just SHOW them!"

He pushed a button on the podium.

I screamed as the floor dropped away.

I fell hard and fast.

I saw the others falling beside me.

My hands flew up as I dropped straight down . . . screaming . . . screaming all the way.

7

"AAAAIIIIIIII!"

I landed hard on my elbows and knees. Pain shot through my body.

I let out another cry as someone landed on top of me. My face sank into a deep carpet.

Groaning, I raised my head and glanced around.

We had all landed in a pile. A tangle of arms and legs and bodies.

Groaning, I scrambled to my knees. My neck throbbed. My back ached. My heart was fluttering. I took a deep breath and held it.

You're okay, Lizzy. You're okay.

At least we landed on a soft, thick rug. Someone grabbed my hand. Matt. He tugged me to my feet.

I saw my brother, Luke, still on his knees. He shook his head, dazed.

I helped pull him up. Then I helped some other kids.

No one spoke. We had fallen to the floor below. But everyone seemed to be okay.

I glanced around the large room. I saw rows of black seats. A gray curtain at the front of the room began to slide open. I could see a movie screen behind it. A screening room.

"Seats, everyone!" The deep voice of The Menace rang out from a loudspeaker beside the screen. "Take your seats. The movie is about to begin."

And then I heard The Menace's high, shrill voice: "So sorry there's no popcorn. But you probably won't mind. I don't think you'll be too hungry after you see this movie! Hahahaha!"

What an ugly laugh.

My legs were shaky. My stomach still felt tight, as if I'd swallowed a heavy rock.

Luke and I walked together. We took seats in the second row.

I sank into the chair. It felt warm and soft. It was *furry*!

I started to lower my hands to the chair arms — but the arms *moved*!

The chair arms lifted up — and wrapped themselves tightly around my waist.

I started to struggle — but something made me stop.

I went limp and listened hard. Yes! I could hear the chair breathing. I could feel it pulsing all around me.

The chair was ALIVE!

Warm and breathing and alive. Its arms held me down.

I sank into the moist fur. It smelled like my dog when she needs a bath.

"It . . . it's a living creature!" Luke whispered. "Lizzy, this is too creepy."

"Enjoy the film, everyone," The Menace boomed. "A little history lesson. And also . . . a preview of some of the *horrible* things that I have planned for you!"

The red face spoke up: "And, people, please don't close your eyes during the scary parts. The Fear Meter is running. You know what that means. We need you to be afraid every moment. You can do it, guys. I know you can!"

The ceiling lights faded. My chair let out a soft growl. I could feel its heart pulsing steadily.

Another chair growled. I turned to Luke. Even in the darkness, I could see the fear on his face.

Carly Beth and Sabrina sat in front of us. Carly Beth's chair had its arms wrapped over her arms. She couldn't move.

The movie started. Black and white, like everything in Panic Park.

It focused slowly. I saw a roller coaster. The sound came on. Kids on the roller coaster, screaming and laughing.

The camera was in a roller coaster car. The car roared up a steep climb, picking up speed.

And as I watched it rise, my chair *took off.*

I felt it shoot up off the floor. Growling softly, it floated higher, picking up speed. Higher, toward the dark ceiling of the theater.

Was this one of those fake rides where your chair jerks you all around, and you pretend you're flying?

No.

We were all really up in the air. I could see the floor far below.

I screamed as the chair tilted one way, then the other. I saw what was happening. Our chairs were all tilting with the kids in the movie coaster.

I tilted back. The arms gripped me tighter. I couldn't move. I couldn't breathe.

The chairs all tilted down and sank fast. Our screams joined the screams of the kids in the movie.

My chair twisted me one way, then the other. And then, with a *whoosh*, it lifted me up again.

I flew high, then came roaring down, squealing down, *shooting* down.

Bumping and bucking. I felt the chair's heart pounding with mine. Felt its furry arms tighten. Listened to its soft growl.

And as I stared helplessly at the screen, the coaster car in the movie went *flying off the tracks*.

Kids on the screen squealed in horror.

And I opened my mouth in a terrified wail as my chair went flying out of control across the theater.

Oh, no . . . Oh, nooooo!

I heard a sickening crash in the movie.

My flying chair had spun the wrong way. I couldn't see the movie screen. But I pictured those poor kids . . . pictured them crashing to the ground.

And then my chair started to spin. It whirled faster, like a top. I shut my eyes.

When I opened them, my chair was back on the floor. In the second row behind Carly Beth and Sabrina. I tried to shake off my dizziness. The two girls were trembling, too.

The movie screen went gray.

The voice of The Menace boomed through the loudspeakers. "Well, we went off the tracks there. I hate when that happens — don't you?" He laughed.

His red face chimed in: "That was the beginning of it all. Back in 1974. Things started to go wrong in the park. We lost a few kids that day. Big whoop — right? Win a few, lose a few!"

The movie began again. It showed a tall, narrow stone tower. The tower stretched high above the park.

A sign in front read: TOWER TO NOWHERE.

The camera moved inside the tower. People were climbing stone stairs. The stairs wound around and around.

As I watched them climb, the air in the theater grew warmer.

People leaned forward as they climbed. The steps grew steeper. The people climbed in small circles. The tower seemed to grow even more narrow.

The air grew hotter. Hot and wet. So hot, my nostrils started to burn. Drops of sweat ran down my forehead.

"It's . . . hard . . . to . . . breathe," Luke whispered beside me.

Yes. The air was *suffocating*!

My face burned from the stifling hot air. I began breathing through my mouth. My deep breaths made my chest burn, too.

In the movie, people kept climbing. Jammed together, they kept circling the tower, trudging higher.

The screen went gray again. A spotlight flashed on at the side of the screen.

The Menace stood behind a small podium. His hat rested on the podium shelf. His dark face peered out at us.

"More annoying problems for Panic Park that year," he said. "People climbed to the top of the Tower to Nowhere — and never came back down. We got into a little trouble for that."

He sighed. "No one understood me. My experiments with the outer limits of fear became more and more brilliant. But no one appreciated me."

His head spun around, and his second face snapped at him. "You think you were so brilliant? You were brilliant like an *ox*! I TOLD you the Tower to Nowhere was an *awful* idea. But did you listen to me?"

The head spun around. "Shut up!" the dark face barked. "Shut up! Shut up! When I want your opinion, I'll rattle your cage!"

The head spun again. "You're not too big to SLAP!"

"Who's going to do it? YOU? Please don't make me laugh. I've got chapped lips!"

"Think I can't give you a SLAP that'll set your head spinning?"

"Go ahead. See who it hurts!"

Imprisoned in the chair, I sat staring as the two faces argued. I couldn't move. Could hardly breathe.

The man is a MONSTER, I told myself.

Look at him, fighting with his second face. A monster.

Did he do that to himself? Give himself a second face in his experiments in fear?

He will do anything. Anything . . .

How can we survive a total monster?

The spotlight went out. The movie started again.

I saw a white building. A sign above the entrance read: RIDE THE WHIRLWIND.

The camera went inside. Dark at first. And then the picture brightened, and I saw people in a long tunnel. People being blown off their feet. Lifted by a powerful, roaring wind.

A boy flew across the screen. His shirt had blown over his head. A girl held on to his leg as the wind carried them down the tunnel. Her hair blew high above her head. They were both screaming in horror, helpless in the powerful, raging wind.

And then I felt a burst of cold wind brush my face. Another strong gust blew my hair up high on my head.

A swirling wind blew through the movie theater. Some kids screamed as the wind pressed us back into our living seats . . . pushed against us as if trying to blow us away.

"Can't . . . breathe . . ." The words escaped my throat.

40

And then I heard kids screaming all around me.

"I can't breathe!"

"Stop it! Please — STOP it!"

"Turn it off! Can't you turn it off?"

"Experience The Whirlwind!" The Menace screamed from beside the screen.

I could hear people shrieking and wailing in the movie. But I couldn't see them. My eyes were shut tight against the roaring wind.

"Experience The Whirlwind!" The Menace repeated. He laughed his cold laugh. "Live it! Live it!"

My chest was about to burst. I couldn't suck air in or out. The raging waves of wind were too powerful.

And then I heard The Menace's other face shout: "Stop it, you fool! You've gone too far! You're going to KILL them all!"

The wind stopped.

Gasping for air, I pressed my hands to my frozen cheeks. Then I tried to smooth my hair down.

I could still hear the roar of the wind gusts, rising and falling like ambulance sirens in my ears. I took a long breath and let it out slowly.

"Were you watching the film?" The Menace demanded. "Did you see those people struggling against the winds? They were terrified! It was beautiful! What a beautiful sight!"

The chair pulsed around me. I could feel its heartbeat against my back. Thinking about it gave me the shivers.

"When people stumbled from The Whirlwind," The Menace continued, "their brains were a little scrambled." He sneered. "Big deal — right?"

His head spun, and the bright red face spoke up. "You went too far. You turned their brains to mush!"

"And what's *your* excuse?" the dark face snapped. "Okay, okay. Maybe my experiments with fear and reality went too far. Something went wrong, guys. The Fear Level in the park was so high, it *hurled* us into another reality."

He sighed. "Yes, I closed Panic Park. And then my beautiful park went spinning away . . . whirling away to a parallel universe. The world moved on. The years passed. But we stayed in 1974."

He picked up his hat and twirled it in his hands. "I loved it at first," he said. "It gave me time to do more experiments in fear. My experiments were brilliant. I learned the true path to terror."

The head spun. "A lot of people disappeared because of you," the red face said. "A lot of people became shadows."

The first face spun back. "You can't make chicken soup without breaking a few chickens!" he boomed. "My experiments in fear were exciting. But I got bored. I decided I wanted to return to the real world."

He kept twirling the wide-brimmed hat between his gloved hands. "How to get back? I began studying the problem. And guess what, people? I discovered that HorrorLand park was built on the *same spot* where Panic Park had stood.

"I discovered I could use mirrors to travel

back and forth between Panic Park and HorrorLand. I could travel to HorrorLand through even the *tiniest* mirror. It was an amazing discovery. But then ... I had a little accident."

"Is THAT what you call me?" the red face screamed. "An ACCIDENT?"

"Shut up! Shut up!" the first face cried. He turned back to us. "I was doing an experiment with a two-way mirror. The experiment went wrong. And I ended up with that ugly face attached to my head."

"You're not winning any beauty prizes!" the other face said. "Come on, people. Check out my blue eyes, my adorable blond eyebrows. Let's vote on which of us has the prettiest face."

I looked down the row of kids. No one moved. We were trapped in the pulsing, living chairs. Staring in silent horror at this insane monster with two faces.

"Now I need *your* help, people," The Menace said. "I need your Fear Level to go so high that Panic Park returns to its place in the real world. Fear brought us here, and fear will bring us back."

Michael sat at the end of my row. I could see the anger burning in his eyes. Finally, he spoke up. "No way!" he shouted, swinging his fist at The Menace. "No *way* we'll help you!"

We all started shouting at once. "No way!" Matt shouted. "No way! No way!"

"Let us go!" I cried.

The Menace waved a hand in the air. And I felt my chair arms tighten around my waist. The arms raised themselves to my throat and began to choke off my breath.

Choking, gasping for air, I grabbed the chair arms and struggled to pull them off me.

The Menace waved his hand again — and the chair arms sank back to my sides.

"Save your voices for SCREAMING!" The Menace cried. He turned to the side of the stage. Byron appeared, pushing the tall Fear Meter in front of him.

"The meter is still only at twenty-five," The Menace said. "You people aren't trying!"

Only twenty-five, I thought. *We'll never survive what he has in mind.*

"More fear! More fear!" the red face shouted. "I get all tingly just *thinking* about it!"

His words sent a chilling jolt of fear over the room. The Fear Meter needle jumped a little. We were all afraid. Because we knew he was serious. And crazy.

"Keep your eyes on the Fear Meter, guys," Byron chimed in. His big hand thumped the side of it. "We're going to get that red needle up to the TOP!"

10

Byron led us up a long staircase, then down a winding, dark hall, and up another steep staircase. The windows were caked with dust and thick layers of dirt. Almost no light seeped in.

Rows of grinning skulls gazed up at us, embroidered in the black carpet. Tangles of cobwebs dangled from the ceilings, brushing our faces as we passed by.

Low moans followed us down one hallway. Were those *human* sounds?

I shuddered and stayed close to Luke.

We walked in silence. I knew we were all thinking the same thought: *Will we ever get out of this terrifying old mansion alive?*

Door after door revealed only darkness. One wall was filled from top to bottom with hideous, grinning animal heads. Another wall had a collection of thin, rubbery things nailed to it. They looked like *human tongues*!

My stomach heaved. I turned away from the ugly sight.

We climbed another endless stairway. Then Byron led us into the bright light of a huge room.

My eyes adjusted slowly. When I could focus, I saw wooden tables and chairs. Several rows of bunk beds against one wall. A bathroom. Two long wooden benches under narrow, dirt-stained windows.

A brick fireplace took up one wall. I squinted hard. Were those *bones* piled on the fireplace floor?

An enormous painting of The Menace, in a flowery silver frame, stared at us from above the fireplace. His hat was pulled over one eye. The other eye glared coldly. The rest of his face was lost in shadow.

I shuddered. A Fear Meter stood against the wall to the right of the bunk beds.

"This is your room," Byron said. "Make yourselves at home."

"Is there room service?" Matt joked. He always put on a brave face.

"Yes," Byron replied. "And a maid will come to turn down your beds and leave chocolates on your pillows at night." He laughed. "What's wrong? No one else is laughing? I don't blame you."

"Byron, how could you work for that . . . that creep?" Carly Beth demanded.

Byron shrugged. "It's not a bad job," he said. "Especially if you like to see kids scream and cry. And think how powerful I'll be when Panic Park returns to the real world!"

He shook his head. "Good luck, guys. You're going to *need* it!"

He disappeared out the door.

Two seconds later, he was back. He came striding up to Matt with his paw outstretched.

"Give it back," Byron said.

Matt stared at him. "Excuse me?"

"Give me back the key card I gave you when you first arrived at HorrorLand. The card that got you into all those locked places."

"No way I'm giving it to you," Matt said. He took a step back. "Why *did* you give it to me?"

A smile spread over the Horror's fur-covered face. "Why? I told you. To make you start thinking about Panic Park," Byron said. "You know. A little clue. To get you interested."

Byron waved his paw in front of Matt's face. "Give it back. Now."

Matt sneered at him. "No way, Furball."

An ugly roar escaped Byron's throat. "Tough talk, Matt my lad," he growled.

His eyes turned fiery red. He balled his big paws into tight fists. "Don't you know I can TEAR you in two?"

Matt tried to dance out of his path. But the big Horror lunged forward. He grabbed Matt by the

48

front of his T-shirt. "Give the card back," he snarled.

Matt shoved Byron's paws away. "I . . . lost it," he said. "I don't have it. I lost the stupid card."

Byron's fiery eyes locked on Matt. "Oh, really?" He grabbed Matt again — wrapped his paws around Matt's waist and *lifted* him off the floor.

"Let's see if you lost it," Byron rasped. "I hope you're not lying to me, Matty Boy."

"You heard me!" Matt shouted. But his voice trembled. "I lost it! Really!"

"Let's see what falls out of your pockets," Byron said. Then he *flipped* Matt sideways like he was a baton and twirled him.

"IIey —" Matt let out a sharp groan.

Byron held him by the ankles. And started to shake him up and down.

Matt's face turned red. His eyes bulged.

Byron shook him harder, shook him as if he were trying to get salt out of a saltshaker.

"Let's see what you've got, boy," Byron said. "Let's see what tumbles out of those jeans pockets," He shook Matt harder.

"Ohhhhh . . ." Matt uttered a long, low moan.

"Let go of him!" Carly Beth cried. "Stop it!" She grabbed Byron's thick paw and tried to pull it off Matt. She wasn't strong enough to budge him.

Michael and Boone dove at Byron. They grabbed him around the waist and tried to wrestle him down.

But Byron gave one hard shake of his body — and both boys went flying to the floor.

Matt groaned again. His voice vibrated as Byron shook him even harder.

Matt shut his eyes.

"Where is it? Where is it?" Byron demanded. "I can shake your brains loose, boy. This isn't a joke. Where IS that card?"

Carly Beth leaned down to Matt. "Give it to him!" she screeched. "Matt — listen to me! Please! Give him the card! Make him stop!"

Matt's face was tomato red. His eyes were shut. His tongue flapped out of his mouth.

Byron shook him, shook him harder.

Panic tightened my throat. "Stop it! Stop it!" I choked out. "Stop it!"

The big Horror slammed Matt's head into the floor.

Matt's eyes rolled up into his head.

Ignoring our cries, Byron shook him some more.

11

"Whoooooah." Matt let out a long groan. He opened his eyes. "Okay." His voice came out in a whisper. "Okay. Okay. You win."

Byron gave him one last shake. Then he set him down on his back and let go of Matt's ankles.

Matt lay sprawled on the floor for a long moment. Finally, he stretched his arms, then his back. He raised his head slowly, blinking hard.

"So dizzy . . ." he murmured. He pressed both hands to his forehead. "Ow. What a headache."

Abby and Julie dropped beside him. "Can you stand up?" Julie asked.

"Stop stalling," Byron snapped. He gave Matt a kick in the ankle. "Move it."

The two girls helped pull Matt to his feet. Matt's eyes were still rolling in his head. He leaned on Abby as he reached into his jeans pocket.

"Okay. Here," he said. He pulled the gray card from his pocket.

Byron snatched it from his hand. He ripped it into two pieces and tossed the pieces to the floor.

He grinned at Matt. "Man, you gave up *easy!*" he said. "I thought you'd put up a better fight than *that!* Ever think of changing your name to *Wimp?*"

Matt rubbed his head. "Give me a break," he muttered angrily.

Byron laughed. "You guys will have to be tougher than *that* if you plan to survive Panic Park!"

Chuckling to himself, he stomped out of the room and slammed the door hard behind him.

Matt staggered to one of the long benches and sat down, rubbing his head some more. The rest of us gathered in front of him.

"Do you believe that guy?" Matt muttered. "I'd like to shake him . . . make his fur fly!"

Billy Deep moved beside me. I could barely see him. His body was made of smoke. It billowed as he moved. His eyes peered out from the shadow.

"I don't feel so well," he told his sister, Sheena. His voice sounded soft and far away. "I feel so . . . cold, Sheena. I can't feel my hands or my feet."

"We'll get you back to normal," Sheena told him. She looked away. "I hope."

"We made a terrible mistake," Julie said, tugging at the ends of her hair. "We were so desperate . . . so desperate to escape HorrorLand and get to Panic Park. But it was all just a trap."

Michael stepped up beside Matt's bench and turned to face us. His expression was angry. He was breathing hard.

"Okay, okay. Now we know about Jillian and Jackson," he said. "And Byron. Who ELSE is a spy for The Menace?"

His eyes moved slowly from face to face. "We trusted those three," he said, "and they were traitors. Who *else* is a traitor? Who *else* is working for The Menace?"

He raised a fist. "Who else?"

Then he stepped up to me and bumped me back with his chest. "Who else is a spy?" he shouted angrily.

"Michael, stop —" I pleaded.

He bumped me again with his chest, forcing me back. "Who else? Who else, Lizzy? How about you and your brother? How about it? How about it?"

12

"No. Please —" I choked out.

Michael bumped me again.

"Leave her alone!" Luke shouted. "We're not spies!"

Michael spun around and leaned over Luke. "We don't know you," he shouted. "You're not Special Guests. You arrived just in time to follow us to Panic Park."

Boone stepped up beside Michael. He scowled at me. "Michael is right. Why are you and your brother here? You're working for The Menace — aren't you!"

"You're WRONG!" I screamed. I shoved Michael back. "You're wrong about Luke and me. We're the ones who tried to *warn* you — remember?"

They stared at me. Michael lowered his fists.

"I tried to warn you about Panic Park," I said. "I said we should all stay in HorrorLand. But then Jillian pretended to read my mind. Remember? She said I was lying."

Luke chimed in: "*Now* we all know who was lying. It was Jillian. So leave my sister alone."

Michael angrily gazed around the room. "Who else is a spy? Who else is a traitor?"

Carly Beth grabbed him by the shoulders. "Michael, listen to me," she said softly, calmly. "We're in terrible danger. We have to trust each other."

"She's right," her friend Sabrina said. "We can't stand here arguing and turning on each other. We have to get out of here!"

Michael grumbled to himself. Then he let out a sigh and dropped beside Matt on the bench.

"We're in a horrible jam," Carly Beth said. "If we survive The Menace's scares, he *wins*. Panic Park returns to the real world. Imagine the terrible things he could do then!"

"But what choice do we have?" Robby asked. "NOT to survive?"

"If we survive, we help him," I said. "And if we *don't* survive . . . we're DEAD."

"There's one more choice," Matt said. "We get OUT of here."

He jumped to his feet. "If we *escape* Panic Park, The Menace loses!" he said. He pointed to the Fear Meter against the wall. "If we can get ourselves back to HorrorLand before that meter hits one hundred, The Menace loses big-time. His park is stuck here in 1974."

"But *how*?" Sheena asked in a trembling voice. "How can we escape? Look at my brother. Billy is a shadow. If The Menace can do something like that to us, how can we ever hope to escape?"

"Matt is totally right," Michael said, jumping up. "So The Menace is powerful. And evil. And crazy. That doesn't mean we just sit here and wait for him to terrify us. We've got to ACT!"

Matt bolted toward the door. "Let's go."

"It's probably locked," Carly Beth said. "And The Menace is probably listening to every word we say."

"We've got to try," Matt said.

We trotted after him. He grabbed the brass doorknob. Twisted it and pulled.

The door swung open.

"Not locked!" Carly Beth cried. "Did Byron forget?"

"Or is it a trap?" Julie asked.

Her words sent a chill down my back. But I knew we didn't have a choice.

Matt stepped out into the hall. I took a deep breath — and followed him.

13

The long, dark hall stretched both ways. The skulls stitched in the carpet stared up at us. The dirt-caked windows let in an inky gray light. The air was hot and smelled musty and sour.

We didn't walk — we ran.

Our shoes thudded on the thick carpet. We hurtled down one long hall, turned, and ran down another.

"We're up high," Michael said breathlessly. "We have to find a stairway down to the first floor."

We turned another corner. No sign of any stairs. We ran past a tall mirror, cracked down the middle.

I pressed my hand against the glass. It was hard. Not an escape route.

"Oh, wow," Carly Beth muttered from up ahead. I followed her gaze.

A TV monitor hung from the ceiling. It showed the Fear Meter. The red line had climbed to 40.

The bracelet on my wrist was tingling. I felt it grow warm against my skin.

"We have to stay calm," I said. "We can't let our Fear Level climb."

"Stay calm?" Abby cried. "Are you CRAZY?"

Matt gave her a gentle push. "Keep moving," he said. "Don't look at any TV monitors. Don't pay any attention to that meter. Just keep going."

Matt led the way. We started to jog again. Down another long, straight hall.

A black cat sat hunched in the middle of the carpet.

No. Not a black cat. As I trotted closer, I saw that it was a *shadow* cat. It floated just above the carpet, gray eyes peering out at us.

It uttered a sad *meow* as we ran past.

At the end of the hall, I saw two shiny doors.

"A dead end," Carly Beth gasped. "We have to go back."

"No. Wait," Matt said. "Check it out." He pointed to a button at the side of the two doors. "It's an elevator."

"It'll take us down," Boone said. He wiped sweat off his forehead with the sleeve of his T-shirt. "Maybe it'll take us to the basement, and we can sneak out."

We stared at the shiny double doors in silence.

Matt pushed the button. Once. Twice.

The doors slid open slowly. We stared into the elevator car. It was narrow and deep. The walls were solid black. A single light-bulb cast a triangle of dim light from the low ceiling.

We jammed into it, all sixteen of us. The car rocked a little under our weight. We pressed together. Too nervous to speak.

The doors squeaked as they slid shut. As the doors slammed together, the light went out.

"Oh, no!" I cried. My heart skipped a beat.

Kids groaned and gasped.

Total darkness.

"Not much air in here," Julie said behind me. "It's getting hot already!"

"Lizzy, you're in front," Abby said. "Push the button."

I stabbed my hand forward and hit the wall. I ran my hand up and down beside the door.

"Push it," Boone called. "It . . . it's getting really hard to breathe."

"I . . . can't find it," I said. I slid my palm over the elevator wall. I tried the wall on the other side of the doors. I began groping the wall frantically.

"I can't find it. I can't find it!"

"There has to be a down button," Abby said. "I . . . I don't like this. I don't like closed-in places. I . . . feel . . . sick. Please —"

"Open the doors!" Sheena cried. "Let's just get *out* of this thing!"

"Please. I'm going to be sick," Abby moaned.

Luke was pressed beside me. In the darkness, he began feeling the wall, searching for a button.

I slid my hands over the doors. I searched everywhere.

"There's no button," I said. "No way to move. No way to get out."

"Are we trapped in here?" Abby's voice cracked. She reached over me and started to pound the door with both fists. "No! Let us out! Somebody — let us OUT!"

14

Shouting frantically, Abby pounded the door.

I gasped as the elevator bumped — then started to go down.

Then I let out a startled cry as the floor seemed to drop away from under me.

I stumbled back against Carly Beth and Sabrina. Kids screamed. We were rocked from side to side.

The elevator whirred as it dropped faster . . . faster . . .

I felt my ears pop.

We were dropping . . . sinking like a stone . . . *too fast*. Falling hard . . . harder.

"We're going to CRAAAAASH!" Sabrina shrieked in my ear.

I squeezed Luke's shoulder. Was that ME screaming?

I shut my eyes. My ears popped again.

My knees folded.

I held my breath — and waited for the pain of the crash.

The elevator hit the bottom with a deafening *THUD*. The car rocked hard. Bounced up. Then slammed down again.

I screamed as the force of the fall dropped me to my knees. Kids were groaning and crying.

"Owwww!" Someone's elbow slammed into my back. I toppled forward.

The light flashed back on.

"At least we're alive," Robby groaned from the back of the car.

We quickly scrambled to our feet. My back hurt. I was breathing hard.

"Open the doors," Abby said. "Please ... hurry. I'm going to puke."

I slammed the doors with my open hands. Squinting in the dim light, I searched again for the elevator button.

I couldn't find *anything*.

"Let *me* try!" Michael said, pushing to the front. He balled his fists and pounded with his monster strength.

The doors didn't budge.

"It's getting so hot in here," Boone said. "I feel ... dizzy. Kind of faint."

Billy spoke up. "I'm just a shadow. Maybe I can slip out through a crack and open it from the outside."

He floated like a cloud to the front. Michael stepped out of the way, stumbling over Sabrina.

Billy floated to the top of the doors, then slowly down again. "No crack," he said softly. "No opening anywhere for me to slip through."

Matt raised one hand in the air to get attention. "My bracelet is vibrating," he said. "We have to stay calm. We don't want the Fear Meter to shoot up."

"Calm? How can we stay calm?" Julie cried.

"I don't BELIEVE we're trapped in a stupid elevator!" Michael shouted. He slammed the wall with his fist.

And a metal panel fell off the wall. It revealed a hidden slot.

"A slot for a key card!" Matt exclaimed. "Move out of the way, Lizzy. I'll try my card."

I gasped. "But . . . you gave it to Byron. We all saw you!"

"Oh, yeah. For sure," Matt replied, rolling his eyes. "Are you kidding me? I gave him my library card from back home. The big jerk never even looked at it!"

He tugged the key card from his jeans pocket. He raised it to the slot — and slid it in.

Nothing happened.

15

I felt my stomach tighten. I stared at the elevator doors. No one spoke.

Every second seemed like an hour.

Finally, I heard a soft hum — and the doors slid open.

Some kids cheered. I started to laugh. Crazy, tense laughter.

I darted out of the elevator. Luke nearly tripped me, stumbling out beside me. We all bolted out of there as fast as we could.

Where were we? I gazed around.

We were outside. Staring into the gray sunlight. Standing in the shadow of a back wall of The Menace's mansion.

"Let's go," Matt said.

He didn't have to say any more. We all took off running. We were desperate to get as far from the mansion as we could.

We ran back into the park, which was as grim and gray as before. I could see the Ferris wheel in the distance, black against the gray sky. We ran past dead, empty shops . . . silent rides . . . abandoned food carts.

"Where are we going?" Carly Beth asked. "We need a plan."

Before anyone could answer her, a shadow person floated in front of us.

She was so gray and misty, it took me a few seconds to recognize her. The little girl. The sad little girl shadow we'd seen when we arrived.

She held both hands up to Carly Beth. "Find me," she said in a tiny whisper I could barely hear. "Can you find me? Can you find me?"

Carly Beth let out a sigh. She reached for the girl. She tried to wrap her arms around her and hug her.

"Can you find me?" the little girl cried.

Another shadow appeared. Another little girl. "Can you find me, too? Do you know where I am? Can you hug me, too? Can you hug me, too?"

Another shadow floated next to her. And then four or five more shadows swept around Carly Beth.

"A hug . . . a hug . . . a hug . . ." they all whispered.

Frightened, Carly Beth staggered back. "No, please —" she started.

But the shadow people swarmed over her.

"A hug . . . a hug . . . a hug . . ."

"Carly Beth —" I called to her. I couldn't see

her. She was buried behind the whispering shadows.

"Can you find me?"

"Can you hug me?"

"A hug . . . a hug . . . Please! A hug!"

They covered her in a curtain of heavy shade.

I froze, staring at the swarming shadows. All chanting and pleading so sadly.

And then Carly Beth's scream rose over the muffled voices. "HELP me! HELP me! Get them OFF me! They're SMOTHERING me!"

16

I froze. Carly Beth screamed again.

As I stared in horror, Matt, Robby, and Sheena leaped at the shadows. They struggled to pull them off her.

"A hug . . . a hug . . . a hug . . ." The shadows' frightening chant didn't stop.

The three kids swiped frantically at the shadows, struggling to pull them off Carly Beth.

But it was like trying to grab clouds. Their hands sank into the shadows and slid right through them.

Matt, Robby, and Sheena stepped back, shaking their heads.

Still chanting, the shadows finally drifted away. The little girl was the last to leave. She tossed back her head and let out an ugly cackle.

Then she floated away, too —

—and I screamed. "Oh, NOOOOOOO!"

Carly Beth floated darkly in front of our horrified eyes. A shadow. Carly Beth was lost . . . lost in shadow . . . a shadow person, too.

She raised her hands and stared at them. "Oh, no," she murmured. "Oh, please . . . no."

Billy floated to her side. They stood together, two gray shadows. "We'll be okay," he said. His voice seemed to come from far away. "We'll be okay, Carly Beth, when we get out of this park." And then he added in a tiny voice, "I hope."

Inside her misty cloud, we could see her shadowy body trembling. Her head was down.

"I feel so . . . light and faint," she said. "I can't see you too well. It's like . . . you're all standing in a thick fog."

"It's very cold," Billy said. "I can never warm up. But we'll be okay."

Carly Beth tried to rub her arms. "I can't feel my skin!" She let out a sob. *"I can't feel my skin!"*

Sabrina stepped up close to Carly Beth. "You fought evil before," she told her. "You defeated the Haunted Mask, Carly Beth. You can defeat this, too."

Carly Beth didn't answer. She just kept rubbing her arms, smoke rubbing smoke.

"Hey!" Robby suddenly cried out. He was staring at Britney and Molly. "I just remembered something," he said.

They turned to him. Britney and Molly looked like sisters. They both had coppery hair and brown eyes. Molly was taller and more serious, like an older sister.

"You remembered something about *us*?" Britney asked.

Robby nodded. "You two already made the trip from Panic Park to HorrorLand," he said. "Don't you remember? You came to the game arcade. I was in trouble there."

Britney scrunched up her face, thinking hard. "Yes," she said finally. "Yes, I kind of remember . . ."

"You came back to HorrorLand," Robby said. "You tried to get me to come with you — to Panic Park."

"Yes. Yes, we did," Molly said. "My memory . . . it's weird. It seems like it happened a long time ago."

"Well, how did you do it?" Robby demanded. "Think hard. You've *got* to remember. How did you get out of Panic Park? How did you get to HorrorLand that night?"

The two girls stared at each other. I could see they were concentrating, trying to remember.

"That's so weird," Britney muttered. "I don't remember . . ."

"I can't remember, either," Molly said, shaking her head. "How did we get back to HorrorLand?"

"Keep thinking," Robby urged. "Come on — you can do it. You can remember."

"I . . . I remember it was very windy," Britney said.

"Windy?" Molly said. "Yes, I think you're right. I remember my hair blowing all over. I had to shut my eyes. Yes. It was windy."

"I remember we walked through a building," Britney said, thinking hard. "A white building. Like that one over there, maybe."

She pointed. We all turned and gazed at a low white building with a flat black roof. It had a dark window beside an open door. I didn't see any sign in front. Nothing to tell what was inside.

"Yes, it looked just like that," Britney said. "I think."

"Should we check it out?" Robby asked.

No one answered. We were already walking toward the building.

We stopped outside the open door. Dark inside. Too dark to see what was in there.

"It's like a little house," Matt said. He frowned. "Why would there be a little house in the middle of Panic Park?"

"Are you sure the building you used to escape looked like this?" Robby asked Britney and Molly.

Britney scrunched up her face again. "I . . . I think so . . ." she stammered.

70

Molly nodded. "It's so hard to remember. Maybe . . . maybe The Menace messed up our memories."

"Let's go in," Michael said. He didn't wait for anyone to argue. He stepped into the doorway and strode into the building.

The rest of us followed close behind him.

"It's a waiting room," I said as soon as my eyes adjusted to the dim light. I saw a few chairs, a couch, a table with a stack of magazines, a reception counter behind a glass window.

A doctor's waiting room.

A thick layer of dust covered everything. I picked up some magazines from the table. The pages were yellowed. The magazines were all from 1974.

"Ohhh, yuck," Abby moaned.

She was staring at a fish tank in the wall. The goldfish in the tank were just bones — skeletons floating on their sides.

"No one has been here for years," Luke muttered.

And then a voice shouted from the reception desk. "The doctor will see you now!"

Huh?

A man in a totally weird superhero costume burst into the waiting room.

"Oh, no!" Robby cried. "It's Dr. Maniac!"

17

"You . . . you followed us from HorrorLand?" Robby cried.

Dr. Maniac pushed back his leopard-skin cape. He wore red-and-blue tights and a red-and-gold top. His gloves and boots were bright yellow.

His eyes rolled crazily behind his red mask. "Did you really think you could escape The Keeper?" he cried.

"Why are you here?" Robby demanded. "Why did you follow us?"

"Because I'm a MANIAC!" he exclaimed. He tossed back his head and laughed a shrill, hyena laugh.

Matt took two long strides toward Maniac. "Leave us alone!" he shouted.

Maniac gave Matt a crooked grin. "Which hand do you butter your bread with?" he demanded.

"Excuse me?" Matt squinted at him.

"Which hand do you butter your bread with? Your left hand or your right hand?"

Dr. Maniac didn't wait for an answer. "That's funny," he said. "I don't use my hand. I use a butter knife!" Again, he tilted his head back and uttered a long, high laugh.

"You're not funny!" Robby cried angrily. "I created you. I drew you. You're a comic book character that I made up!"

"I made YOU up!" Maniac declared. "If I shut my eyes, I can make you disappear! Ha!"

"Tell us how to get out of this park," Matt demanded. "Tell us what we have to do."

"Can you stand on your head and whistle "Dixie" with a mouthful of crackers?" Maniac asked.

Matt turned to Robby. "He isn't going to help us. Let's get out of here."

"Oh, but I *am* going to help you," Dr. Maniac said, moving to block the door. The leopard-skin cape fluttered in front of him. He pushed it out of his way.

He moved to the wall and opened a cabinet door. On the cabinet shelf stood a Fear Meter. The red line was just above 50.

"Tsk-tsk," the supervillain clucked. "Look at that fear *climb*. You're halfway there. I'll bet all that fright is making you hungry and thirsty. Follow me."

"We're not following you — we're leaving!" Matt cried.

I went to the door with Matt. But we all stopped when we saw the shadow people.

At least a dozen of them. Floating in the doorway. Waiting for us.

The room grew icy cold as they moved in, spreading their shadowy arms. They swarmed around us silently.

I felt their icy touch on my skin. And then a thick curtain of darkness lowered over me.

They were forcing us to move . . . forcing us to walk . . . holding us prisoner in their foggy grip.

I shivered when the shadows pulled away. We were standing in front of a small diner. Through the window, I could see a long lunch counter with stools lining the front.

A gray neon sign flickered over the glass door. The sign read: SHAKE SHACK.

The shadow people forced us inside. The door slammed shut behind us.

I gazed around. The walls were covered with large posters of hamburgers and milk shakes in tall glasses.

Beneath his red mask, Dr. Maniac had a wide grin on his face. "Everyone here?" he shouted. "Okay. Enjoy your shakes!"

He moved to a lever near the door and pulled it down.

I heard a low hum. The hum grew louder.

74

"Hey!" I felt the floor lift up. No — wait. The *whole restaurant* was rising.

Kids cried out as the walls started to vibrate. The floor shook — gently at first, then harder.

The diner tilted hard to the left. Kids stumbled to the wall. Michael and Julie fell to the floor. I struggled to keep my balance.

But the room rocked the other way. And then the whole diner started to shake.

I screamed and tried to grab on to Luke. But we both fell to the floor.

Before we could scramble up, the room tilted sharply — and we tumbled into the wall.

I let out a cry as my arm smashed against the solid plaster. Pain shot up my arm . . . my neck.

Kids were shrieking and crying out as the room shook harder.

"It's . . . like an EARTHQUAKE!" Sabrina cried. She grabbed my shoulder. We tried to balance. But another jolt sent us crashing into Matt and Boone.

I turned and saw Dr. Maniac floating calmly above the rattling, vibrating floor. "Nothing like a good SHAKE!" he exclaimed. Then he laughed his ugly, shrill laugh.

"Owwww!" I let out another cry as Michael stumbled into me. We both slammed against the wall.

"I think I broke my arm!" someone wailed.

"Stop! I'm so . . . dizzy!" Julie yelled.

Another hard jolt — up, then down — and we bounced like rubber balls on the floor.

My stomach lurched. I felt sick.

I pressed my hand over my mouth. Tried to force my stomach to stop heaving. And my head slammed against the wall again.

I dropped to my knees. My knees bounced hard on the quaking floor.

"STOP it!"

"PLEASE! STOP!"

"That's the way the ball BOUNCES!" Maniac cried. Then he tossed back his head and giggled at the trembling ceiling.

"NOOOOO!" Boone screamed as his head rammed into the wall. He bounced on the floor, eyes shut in pain, holding his head.

Shaking against the wall, Abby's knees buckled. She leaned over the floor and puked loudly.

I staggered from side to side. Looking up, I saw Maniac's eyes on me.

"OH!" I felt a jolt from his hard stare.

And I went flying backward. My head smacked the counter. Pain shot down my body.

I saw stars. I actually saw stars.

And then everything faded to black.

18

"Lizzy — wake up. Wake up."

I heard Luke's voice. It sounded very far away.

Slowly, I opened my eyes, groaning from the pain. Luke was on his knees beside me. His hands were on my shoulders. "Are you okay?"

"I . . . I guess." My voice came out in a hoarse whisper.

I sat up. Slowly, the room came back into focus. The shaking had stopped.

Kids were sprawled everywhere. They looked dazed, in pain. Boone still had his hands pressed against the top of his head. Matt stood doubled over against the counter.

Carly Beth and Billy hovered close together in the middle of the room. Still shadows, they had faded to a pale gray, like smoke from a dying campfire.

Julie and Abby had their backs against the lunch counter. Both girls were trembling hard.

Their knees quivered. Their arms were shaking. I could hear their teeth chattering.

"I . . . I can't stop . . . sh-shaking!" Julie stammered.

They both hugged themselves tightly. But their whole bodies trembled as if the room was still going crazy.

Dr. Maniac laughed at them. "That's a really BAD case of the shakes!" he cried. His grin faded. "Don't worry, girls. If you DIE, you'll probably stop shaking after a few weeks in the grave!"

Abby moaned. "I . . . I . . . I . . ." She was trembling too hard to talk.

Maniac laughed again.

Robby climbed unsteadily to his feet. He held his arms out, trying to balance. He stumbled toward Dr. Maniac.

"I created you!" Robby shouted angrily. "I drew you in my comic strip. And I know how to destroy you!"

Dr. Maniac raised a long gloved finger and picked his nose with it. "That's what I think of your threat."

"Help us get out of here," Robby said. "Help us — and I'll let you live!"

Maniac picked his nose some more, his eyes on Robby. "Think you're a big-deal comic-book art-ist?" he said, sneering. He moved behind the lunch counter. "I'm an artist, too, Robby Boy. Watch this."

He pulled up a large paintbrush. He carried it over to Robby. "I like to work with a brush," he said. "Just like you. Watch an artist at work!"

He swept the brush over Robby's face — and Robby's face disappeared.

I gasped as the Maniac smoothed the brush over Robby's neck. Down the front of his chest.

With each stroke, part of Robby vanished!

In a few seconds, the supervillain had brushed Robby away.

"How do you like my brushwork?" Dr. Maniac bellowed. "You taught me everything I know! HAHAHAHA!"

I stared in horrified silence. Stared at the spot where Robby had stood.

I couldn't hold myself in. I screamed, "Robby — are you there? Are you still there?"

And then I turned to the grinning Maniac — and cried, "What have you DONE to him?"

19

Dr. Maniac didn't answer me. He stood there waving his paintbrush in the air. "Would anyone else like me to do their portrait?" he cried. He was staring right at me.

The room grew silent.

Maniac dropped the brush to the floor. He walked to the lunch counter. He bent over and pulled something out from behind it.

A Fear Meter.

My breath caught in my throat. The red line had risen to 75.

Maniac gazed at the screen. "Very good," he muttered. "Good work, guys."

He turned to us. "Lots of fear here in my little diner. I guess I've done my job well. Bye-bye, everyone!"

He tossed his cape behind him and hurried out the door.

"Robby? Are you still here?" I tried again.

"Can't you see me?" Robby's voice sounded tinny, far away. "I'm here. Can't you see me?"

Then he let out a moan of horror. "Ohhhhhh. My hands. I can't see my hands. I . . ."

We stared in silence at the spot where the voice came from.

Robby wailed at the top of his voice. "What did he DO to me? I can't see myself! What did he DO to me?"

"We can hear you," I told Robby. "You're still here. But you're invisible. We'll get you back. I *know* we will."

Carly Beth and Billy floated around the spot where Robby stood. Their shadowy faces couldn't hide their fear.

"Look at us!" Matt cried. He waved his arm around the room. "Look what The Menace has done to us!"

I followed Matt's gaze. Robby was invisible. Carly Beth and Billy were shades. Julie and Abby hugged themselves, unable to stop trembling.

Boone shook his head. "I know we're all trying to be brave and tough it out," he said. "But . . . maybe we WON'T survive. Maybe we're not going to make it."

"We *have* to survive," I said. "The Menace needs to keep us *alive* — right?"

"She's right," Sabrina agreed. "The Menace

wants us to hit one hundred on the Fear Meter. So he *has* to keep us alive. As long as we haven't reached one hundred yet, he has no choice. He has to keep us alive."

"*Some* of us," Robby muttered.

"Robby, stop talking like that. We can't give up," Carly Beth said. "Our only chance is to get out of Panic Park."

Matt helped Abby and Julie to their feet. They could barely stand, their legs were wobbling so hard. Their teeth chattered. Hugging themselves, they took a few shaky steps.

We made our way out of the Shake Shack. In the park, the sky was solid gray as always. The shadow people had disappeared. I didn't see anyone around.

We started walking, keeping close together. We passed more empty shops . . . all dark and silent . . . a game room . . . a small park with withered, bare trees.

Michael led the way. He stopped and pointed. "Another white building," he said. He turned to Britney and Molly. "Could that be the one you escaped from?"

The girls shook their heads. "Maybe."

We walked closer. The building had a stained glass window, all shades of gray and black. The door was shaped like an arch.

"It looks like a church or something," Luke said. "But that can't be right."

A sign on the wall beside the door read: WHAT A SHAME.

We stared at it, shaking our heads. What could that *mean*?

Only one way to find out.

We stepped through the arch into the open doorway. We were in another long, narrow room. Rows of wooden seats filled the center. Candles along both sides provided the only light.

I heard solemn organ music from the far wall. It sounded like funeral music. The deep notes made the walls vibrate.

"It *is* some kind of chapel," I whispered to Luke. "Weird."

We stepped in farther to examine the walls. They were covered with photographs. The photos were all of kids about our age.

Row after row of small framed photographs. Under each photo, a little tag had the kid's name.

I read the names as I moved deeper into the chapel. April Smith . . . Travis Newton . . . Carlos Garcia . . .

And under each name, I saw the letters FTD.

"Wow," Luke muttered from beside me. "None of these kids look too happy."

"Why are their pictures on the wall?" I asked. "And what does FTD stand for?"

Suddenly, Sabrina gasped. The sound echoed through the narrow chapel.

"What's wrong?" I asked.

She was staring at a silver plaque on the wall next to a row of kids' photos.

"Sabrina — what's wrong?"

She pressed a hand to her mouth as she read the plaque. Then she turned to us.

"I . . . I see what FTD stands for," she stammered. "It isn't good."

20

Sabrina pointed to a little tag beside one of the unhappy-looking kids' pictures.

I gasped when I read the tag. "FTD stands for *Frightened To Death*," I said.

Kids uttered shocked cries.

I felt the metal bracelet on my wrist tingle and grow warm. It meant my Fear Level was rising. But what could I do? The sad faces on the wall gazed out at me.

"You mean —?" Sheena started.

I waved to the wall of photos. "None of these kids survived The Menace," I said. "Look at the little sign beneath this photo. It says the kids all died when the Fear Meter hit one hundred. They couldn't survive the fear."

Huddled close beside me, Luke sighed. "What makes us think *we* stand a chance?" he demanded.

"Stop it!" Carly Beth cried. She slid up to Luke. "Stop talking like that. Do you think I want to stay a shadow forever?"

Luke jumped back, surprised by her anger.

"We're *going* to survive — even if it hits one hundred," Carly Beth said. "And we're going back home. And we're all returning to normal."

"She . . . she's right," Julie agreed. She was trembling so much it made her voice shake. "We've all had scary times be-before. And we . . . we won. We can d-do it again."

"Let's go," Matt said. He started to the door. "We're not going to get anywhere staring at these photos."

We followed him back outside. The air had grown cooler. The sky was a dark charcoal gray. A flock of blackbirds flew overhead, chattering loudly.

Matt and Michael trotted up beside Britney and Molly.

"Are you sure you can't remember where that building was?" Matt asked them.

"Can't you remember anything else about how you returned to HorrorLand?" Michael demanded.

And then I heard Robby's voice, close by me. "Think hard," he pleaded. "You both came to the arcade. You were going to bring me back with you to Panic Park. . . ."

The two girls shut their eyes, thinking hard.

"It's all a fog," Britney said finally.

"I remember the white building," Molly said. "I remember we walked inside. And then . . ."

She shook her head. "I'm so sorry. It's all a blank."

"Hey, wait!" Sheena cried. "I don't believe it!"

I followed her gaze. She was staring at a tiny building across the path.

It looked familiar. And then I saw the sign over the entrance: HALL OF MIRRORS.

Some kids gasped. Some cheered.

"Yes!" Boone cried, pumping his fists in the air. "That's how we got here! The mirrors will take us back!"

We didn't hesitate. We all started running.

The doors were closed. Was the building locked?

Boone got there first. He spread his hands over the doors and pulled them apart. They slid open easily.

We piled into the long, narrow room. Dark mirrors on both sides.

My heart thudded in my chest as I stared at a long row of my reflections.

"Okay, everyone!" Matt cried. "Into the mirrors!"

I glanced at my brother. He had a frightened look on his face. But he flashed me a thumbs-up.

I took a deep breath — and leaped into the glass.

21

"OWWWW!"

My head smacked hard. My hands slapped the mirror.

The glass was solid.

In the long row of mirrors, I saw kids tumble back, surprised and disappointed.

The room rang out with groans and unhappy cries.

"Well, *that* went well!" Matt tried to make a joke.

But we were all too disappointed to laugh. We stood there, gazing at our dark reflections.

"Oh, no!" I uttered a cry as I heard the doors slam shut.

The long, narrow room grew darker.

Matt and Boone rushed to the door. I watched them struggle to slide it open.

"We're . . . locked in!" Boone cried. "Someone locked us in. We're trapped in here!"

I felt my bracelet tingle and vibrate.

Lizzy, be calm, I told myself. *Be calm.*

But how could I?

My frightened face stared out at me from the mirrors.

And then . . . my face disappeared.

Kids cried out as their faces vanished. The mirrors went black.

"Oh, no," I moaned. I stared at the ugly green mask that popped into the mirror. It looked like one of the masks Carly Beth had battled in the maze.

It rose up in one mirror, then another . . . then another. Until the hideous mask stared out at us all down the row.

Its rubbery lips bobbed up and down as if it were speaking to us.

And then Captain Ben, the one-legged pirate captain, appeared behind the mask. The pirate's evil face grew larger as the mask faded back. He stared out from every mirror, uttering a crooked-toothed laugh.

I screamed as an enormous snake rose up . . . so close . . . so close it appeared ready to leap from the glass. It raised its head and opened its mouth. Snapped its jaws, once. Twice. A hiss escaped its open mouth, the sound pouring like steam through the tiny room.

"Dr. Crawler!" Boone shouted. "I thought he was poisoned. He's still ALIVE!"

Boone pounded the glass. But the gigantic

snake didn't fade away. It shot its head toward us, letting out another frightening hiss.

Then a decaying mummy staggered forward in front of us. Its wrappings were stained and peeling. Haunted eyes peered out from deep in its ragged head.

The mummy reached its arms out stiffly. Grabbing . . . grabbing . . . Trying to escape from behind the glass.

I saw Abby stagger back. "N-no! Please!" she cried.

But there was nowhere to escape it. The mummy filled the mirrors in front of us and behind us.

"It's all our old enemies!" Carly Beth cried. "They're all here! All working for The Menace! All here to frighten us!"

My bracelet. Pain seared up and down my arm as the metal burned into my wrist. The Fear Meter rose in all the mirrors. And they all showed the red line bouncing over 80. Creeping higher . . . higher . . .

"We have to get OUT of here!" Matt shouted.

He tried the doors again. They wouldn't slide open. He lowered his shoulder and heaved himself at them.

No. No way.

I turned back to the mirrors — and saw an evil-looking ventriloquist dummy loom up in all of them. His wooden hair stood up in a tall wave.

His eyes darted wildly from side to side. He had a leering grin on his face. His jaw made a clicking sound as it moved up and down.

"Slappy!" Britney and Molly screamed at once.

"That's MISTER Slappy to *you*!" he screeched.

He could *hear* us!

His evil face filled the mirrors. He turned his eyes on Michael. "Kid, I've got one word of advice for you. DEODORANT." He laughed a tinny laugh.

Then his eyes landed on Matt. "Do you know how to tell your face from your butt? No? Neither do I! HAHAHAHA!"

"You're not funny!" Britney screamed. "What do you want? Why did you follow us here?"

Slappy's mouth clicked open. He leaned forward, peering out at Britney with that evil grin. "Britney, I think you're pretty — pretty ugly! Ha-ha. I love your nose. Do you open bottle caps with it? Ha-ha."

His eyes darted from side to side. "And where is Robby? Invisible? Ha-ha. Robby, you never looked better! Maybe you should *all* make this a more beautiful world — and DISAPPEAR!"

I stared at the dummy's reflections, my mind spinning. Why was he doing this? Was he just going to make bad jokes?

"You're all going to disappear like Robby!" Slappy cried in his raspy voice. "Your Fear Level is almost to one hundred. That means The

Menace and all of us *good guys* will be returning to earth."

He pressed his wooden face closer. His eyes blinked wide. "And do you really think The Menace will send you back to your mommies and daddies? I don't think so!"

"SHUT UP!" Britney shrieked. "SHUT UP! SHUT UP! I HATE you!"

She smacked her fists against the mirror. Trying to hit him. "I HATE YOU! I HATE YOU!"

Slappy let out a giggle. He raised a wooden hand. He pointed two fingers at Britney. "Let me show you a wonderful trick The Menace taught me!"

I heard a crackling sound. Like an electrical shock.

Britney staggered back. She stumbled into the mirror behind her.

Her eyes bulged. Her mouth hung open, and she took wheezing breaths.

Slappy pointed the two fingers at her again.

Again, I heard the crackle of electric current.

Britney let out a moan.

Something happened to her face. Her mouth froze open. Her eyes stopped moving. Her face appeared to harden.

And then, as I stared in horror, Britney's whole head hardened. Her skin began to glow like polished wood.

"*Unnh unnnh unh.*" An ugly grunt escaped her throat.

She raised a hand and pushed under her chin, struggling to close her mouth. Her mouth made a clicking sound as it closed.

Slappy laughed. He pointed his fingers at her again.

"*Unnh unnnh,*" Britney grunted.

Her eyes darted stiffly from side to side. Her head tilted forward, then back. Her mouth clicked as she tried to speak.

"Ha-ha!" Slappy laughed. "Britney, dear, I always thought you were a DUMMY!"

I was standing right next to Britney. I reached for her.

My hand brushed her head. It was *solid wood*!

Her head was a dummy's head!

Slappy peered out from the long rows of mirrors. "Who *else* would like to join my show?" he shouted.

22

The dummy's laugh roared out from all the mirrors.

Poor Britney gripped her wooden head in both hands. Her mouth clicked open, but no sound came out.

A wave of horror swept down my body. I pressed my back against the glass and took long, slow breaths.

My eyes wandered down the row of terrified kids.

Billy and Carly Beth were shadow people. Robby was invisible. Abby and Julie couldn't stop shaking. And Britney stood there, grunting and tugging at her wooden dummy head.

It's like a horror movie, I thought. And then I told myself: *No. It's like living in TEN horror movies at once!*

"We've got to get out of here," Matt shouted. "Everybody — think!"

"Yes! Why don't you use your brain?" Slappy snapped. "Use it to ram your head against the door! HAHAHAHA!"

Slappy's laugh faded as he sank back in the mirror. I gasped as I saw who appeared next — The Menace.

His black hat was tilted over his face. The collar of his black shirt was pulled up. He looked like a black smudge repeated again and again down the row of mirrors.

"People, people —" he boomed. "You're just not trying."

He tilted his hat back, but his face was still in shadow. I stared down the aisle. There were dozens of Menaces staring back at me.

"People, the Fear Meter is only at eighty," The Menace complained. "Really, guys, I expected more from you."

"Let us out of here!" Michael screamed.

"You can't keep us in here!" Sheena chimed in.

"Let us go! Let us go!" several kids started to shout.

The Menace ignored them. "I guess you don't think I'm serious," he said. "Let me see . . . What can I do to prove to you that I *mean* what I say?"

His head swirled around. His other face appeared. "Why don't you ask *me*? I know how to scare these jerks!"

95

The first face swung back to the front. "I don't think so," he said. "You always go too far. The kids never survive your scares!"

I shuddered. I pictured all those kids' sad faces in the chapel. And the terrifying words: *Frightened To Death.*

"Well . . ." The Menace rubbed his chin with a gloved hand. "Okay. Fine. Go ahead," he said to his other face. "*Kill* some of them if you think it'll get the Fear Meter to the top. Do whatever you want to them. . . ."

23

KILL some of them?

His terrifying words sent chill after chill down my back.

"You're CRAZY!" Michael screamed. He slapped his hand against the mirror.

Matt tried to pull him back. But Michael totally lost it.

"You're crazy! Crazy! CRAZY!" he shouted at the shadowy face in the mirrors. Michael was so angry, the veins were throbbing in his neck. He pounded the mirror again and again.

The Menace watched him calmly. Under the hat, his eyes were narrow slits. "You *are* a brave lad," he told Michael. "Yes, yes. I know you're part monster. I know your whole story, kiddo. It's so impressive the way you stand up to me."

His head spun around. "So impressive, I could puke!" the red face said.

"But really . . . who is crazy here?" the first face said softly. "I think I make perfect sense."

"Just let us go!" Michael screamed. "I don't care if —"

He stopped.

A blinding flash of white light made us all stop.

I shut my eyes. The light was so bright, it sent a burning jolt of pain through my head.

I opened my eyes slowly. And stared in shock at the mirrors.

They all appeared to spin. Spinning faster and faster, until the face in the mirrors was a blur.

Michael opened his mouth in a long wail of horror.

It was Michael's face in the mirrors. Dozens of spinning reflections. Michael's mouth open . . . screaming . . . screaming out his rage in every mirror. Screaming, his eyes bulging, his face twisted in anger, as he spun . . . spun . . .

Then the scream cut off sharply as the mirrors came to a stop. Darkness fell over us.

Silence. A terrified silence down the long room.

And then slowly, the lights brightened. I struggled to breathe. I saw the other kids shaking their heads, blinking, dazed.

And then my eyes stopped on Michael. Michael squinting hard into the mirror in front of him.

And on the back of Michael's head . . . on the back of his head . . . on the back of his head . . .

My heart skipped a beat.

On the back of Michael's head was ANOTHER FACE!

A hideous monster face with bulging eyes and a long lizard snout. Pointed, jagged teeth and a long black forked tongue.

The Menace peered out at Michael from the mirror with a sick grin on his shadowy face. "How's that working for you, partner? Glad you complained?"

24

Michael's second face opened its long snout in a monster growl.

I screamed. I couldn't hold it in.

Some kids stampeded to the exit door and pounded on it frantically.

Michael gazed into the mirror, turning his head from side to side. His eyes were wide with horror, but he didn't say a word or cry out.

"Michael, my boy," The Menace called. "If you act like a monster, you should LOOK like one!" He laughed.

"Good one!" The Menace's other face declared.

Michael just kept twisting his head around. Studying the monster face on the back of his head. Staring as if he didn't believe it.

"Let us out! Let us go!" kids screamed.

The Menace peered out at us from under the shadow of his hat. "I'm enjoying this, people," he said. "I'm feeling it. Yes, I'm *feeling* it! Could you scream a little harder?"

The Fear Meter flashed into the mirrors. I stared at the red line. It was bouncing near 95.

"Almost back!" The Menace cried. "My beautiful park is almost back! I can't wait!"

"What will happen to us?" Carly Beth called. Her voice floated out softly from her shadow. "If we bring your park back, what will happen to *us*?"

The Menace pulled the brim of his hat lower over his face. "You don't really want to ask that question — do you?"

The red face whirled around. "FTD!" it shouted. "FTD! FTD!"

I gasped as gray light flooded the narrow aisle. It took me a few seconds to realize the exit door had opened.

We all stood blinking, gazing at the open door.

"Don't just stand there, people!" The Menace said. "You know how I *get* when I'm kept waiting."

Kept waiting . . .

The last time The Menace was kept waiting, he vacuumed up that shadow person. He killed that person just for being slow.

I shuddered just thinking about it. *Would he do that to us?*

And then suddenly, different thoughts whirred through my brain. . . .

What would happen if we FORCED ourselves to be calm?

101

What could The Menace do if he saw the Fear Meter drop lower and lower?

If he couldn't make us afraid, would he let us go?

No time to think about that. Both of The Menace's faces were screaming at once: "Go out and be afraid! Be VERY afraid! Go! Go! Go!"

We stampeded out the door. Into the eerie, gray light.

"We need a place to hide!" Michael shouted.

His monster face uttered a low grunt.

"Michael is right," Matt agreed. "We need to regroup. We need —"

He stopped. He was staring straight ahead. He let out a sigh.

I turned. I saw the ventriloquist dummy first. Slappy, in his gray suit and red bow tie.

The dummy stood on his own, knees slightly bent, arms dangling at his sides. The painted grin on his lips seemed to spread as he stepped forward.

And then the others came into view. Moving toward us in a line — an ugly line of evil villains we had seen before. But never in one place. Never moving together . . . never moving as one evil force.

Luke huddled close. We all froze with our backs to the Hall of Mirrors. Froze in frightened silence and gazed up and down the line of advancing villains . . .

Dr. Crawler, the venomous snake, with his head raised, snapping his jaws. The snake was wrapped around the arm of Inspector Cranium in his white lab coat.

As if watching a terrifying nightmare, I saw the green lizardlike monsters from the giant eggs staggering toward us. . . . Captain Ben, his wooden leg tapping the pavement, his skeletal pirates behind him.

The ugly, muttering evil mask floated above the others. Beside it, a staggering, ragged mummy. And Dr. Maniac, cape flying, hovered off the ground as he came forward, his yellow-feathered boots kicking the air.

We had no choice. We backed up. Backed up till we were pressed against the wall.

My brother raised his face to me and whispered in my ear. "We're going to be scared to death, just like the kids in that chapel — *aren't* we, Lizzy."

I opened my mouth to answer, but no sound came out.

I saw Abby and Julie at the end of the wall. They couldn't stop trembling. Carly Beth and Billy were gray clouds, fluttering in front of us. Britney held her wooden head in her hands. Tears rolled down her painted cheeks.

"Well, well," Inspector Cranium said, rubbing his hands together. A thin, unpleasant smile spread across his bearded face.

"Well, well. Here we all are. The last chapter."

25

"It's YOUR last chapter!" Matt shouted. "We're not finished yet!"

Dr. Crawler raised himself on Inspector Cranium's arm. "Ssssssave your breath!" he hissed.

Cranium lowered the big snake to the pavement. "You're getting heavy, Crawler," he said. "How many mice did they feed you today?"

"Bite your tongue!" the snake snapped at Cranium.

"Look at you losers," Slappy said, eyes darting from side to side. "Do you really think you stand a chance? Half of you are already shadows or freaks!"

"I'd rather be a freak than a dummy!" Robby yelled.

Slappy's body jiggled as he laughed. "You've got us all beat, Robby. You're an *invisible* freak! Hahaha."

Slappy shook his head. "And you're also a *dummy* — because you created *this* clown!" He pointed to Dr. Maniac.

"I'm not a clown!" Dr. Maniac roared. "I'm a MANIAC!"

He swung around to face Slappy. "I'd grab you and teach you a lesson — but I'd get splinters!"

"Pipe down, ye sea dogs!" Captain Ben boomed, waving his crutch wildly. "If ye sail with me, ye sail as one! It's one for all and all for one. That be the rule of the seven seas!"

The villains all started arguing at once. Dr. Crawler snapped at Captain Ben's wooden leg. The captain brought his crutch down hard on the snake's middle.

"Silence, everyone!" Inspector Cranium cried, waving his hands above his head.

None of us moved. We stayed with our backs to the building wall.

What was this about? Why were the villains so tense? Why were they at each other's throats?

Finally, Cranium got them quiet. He turned back to us. "As I was saying, this is the last chapter. For ALL of us!"

"What do you mean?" I cried. "I ... don't understand. Why is it the final chapter for *you*?"

"Yeah," Luke chimed in. "Don't you work for The Menace?"

Cranium nodded. "Yes, we came to work for The Menace. Byron chose us all. He made us a good offer."

Slappy's mouth clicked up and down. "The Menace said we could all take our revenge on you losers," he rasped. "You know. You got lucky. You defeated us back home. So he gave us another chance."

The snake lifted itself high. "He promissssed us a good time. All we had to do was sssscare you out of HorrorLand. Make you think HorrorLand was unssssafe."

"Aye, and we did a fine job of that," Captain Ben chimed in.

"We made you believe that HorrorLand was the scariest place," Cranium said. "So you would try to escape to Panic Park."

Cranium turned his gaze on me. "It worked, too," he said. "Except that stupid Horror, Ned — he nearly fouled us up by getting you and Luke involved."

"I don't know what you're talking about," I replied. "Who is Ned?"

He rubbed his pointy beard. "Who do you think Monster X was?" Cranium demanded. "Who do you think was desperately feeding you two information about HorrorLand? It was Ned. Monster X was Ned!"

"Ned was trying to help us?" Matt cried.

"How do you know it was Ned?" I demanded.

Cranium shrugged. "I've got my spies. You can't keep a secret from the Thought Police."

"Ha-ha! Cranium is a maniac, too!" Dr. Maniac cried. "Maniacs rule! Maniacs rule!" He did a crazy dance. But he had to stop when his legs got all tangled in his cape.

"Our job was to frighten you out of Horror-Land," Cranium said. "Once we got you to Panic Park, our job was to get your Fear Level to the top. The Menace is very smart. He knew we would be your worst nightmares come true."

"Why are you telling us all this?" I demanded.

"Ssssilence!" Crawler hissed.

"No one can keep a secret from the Thought Police. Not even The Menace. I just read his mind," Cranium continued. "Just now. Just this second. And what I learned, I didn't like."

"What did you learn?" I asked.

Cranium narrowed his eyes. "When you hit one hundred on the Fear Meter and Panic Park returns to the world, he plans to keep you prisoners in the park — forever. And US, TOO!"

"All of us?" I gasped.

"He plans to keep us ALL prisoners," Cranium said. "He's not going to let *any* of us go home after the job is done."

"I . . . still don't understand why you're telling us this," I said.

"Because we need your HELP!" Dr. Maniac screamed.

"Huh?" We all gasped and cried out in surprise.

Slappy shook his head. "I can't believe I'm saying this," he said. "But we have to work together with you losers."

"It's the only way we can defeat him," Cranium said. "The only way we can destroy him."

Matt's mouth hung open. He squinted hard at Cranium and Slappy. "You're joking, right?"

"Let me get this right. You want *us* to help *you* destroy The Menace?" Boone said slowly.

"*You* have to stand up to him!" Cranium said.

Matt laughed. "For sure." He turned to the rest of us. "Don't you get it? It's a trap. A trick. It's the final scare. The final scare that puts the meter over the top. And these guys win."

"No way!" Michael shouted to the row of villains. "No way we help you! No way! No way!"

And we all began to chant: "No way! No way! No way!"

As I chanted along with everyone, I saw the villains' expressions change. I saw the evil settle over their faces. I saw the grim, cold stares as their eyes narrowed.

And I felt chilling fear.

I felt fear freeze every muscle of my body as the villains began to move . . . move in for the final chapter . . . the final attack.

26

We had no place to run.

The villains moved quickly. They pressed us against the building wall.

Slappy's eyes rolled with excitement as he strode stiffly up to me.

Before I could duck away, he pressed his wooden face against my cheek. And rasped in my ear: "We don't like you — and you don't like us. But you freaks are the only ones who can stand up to him."

"Stand up to him?" I asked. "What do you mean? How can *we* stand up to The Menace?"

"You have to show him you have no fear," Cranium replied. "He needs your Fear Energy to keep his park alive. If your Fear Level goes down, The Menace is weakened."

"Stand up to him. Stand in front of him and laugh in his face!" Dr. Maniac declared. He tossed back his head and whinnied like a horse. "Something like that."

"I told you, I read his mind. Here's what I learned. If you all stand in front of him and show no fear," Cranium continued, "The Menace will vanish, and so will Panic Park. If you stare him down, his world will start to shrink. The Menace and the park will grow tinier and tinier — until it's just a memory."

"Hey," Luke chimed in. "If it's so easy, why don't YOU do it?"

"It be far from a job for a fearless pirate," Long Ben answered. "I be feared in all the seventeen seas!"

"Is your leg made of wood — or your head?" Slappy rasped at the pirate. "There are only *seven* seas!"

"I've been places you've never even dreamed of, dummy," the pirate scowled. "One more word against the captain, and I'll be using your head for my anchor!"

"And I'll bite your *other* leg!" Slappy cried, snapping his jaws loudly at Captain Ben.

"Peace! Peace!" Maniac shouted.

Cranium turned back to us. "We can't defeat The Menace," Cranium said. "The Menace isn't measuring *our* fear. He's measuring yours. You are the humans."

He grabbed my wrist and slid his hand over my bracelet. "It's very hot. The Fear Level is high. The Menace is measuring the fear in all of you."

110

"So you losers have to do it," Slappy said. "You have to go back to his mansion. You have to find him. Show him you're not a bit afraid. Make the bracelets go cold."

"Stare him down," Cranium said. "When your Fear Level goes down, he will shrink away. The Menace and Panic Park will shrink away. Once he is tiny and weak, we know how to escape."

"Do it — NOW!" Maniac screamed.

Matt turned to the rest of us. "What do you think?" he asked. "Is this a trap? Can we trust them?"

"No," Michael answered. "We can't trust them. But do we have a choice?"

His second face spun around. "Blah blah blah," it said. It stuck out its long black forked tongue.

Michael's real face spun back. "See what I mean? Look at us. We're totally ruined. Ruined! I think we have to try it. It can't get any worse — can it?"

Famous last words.

27

Inspector Cranium and Dr. Maniac led the way to The Menace's mansion on the other side of the park. The rest of the villains scattered.

We walked in silence past the rides and games and empty restaurants, all colorless and gray.

Did I feel tense?

Three guesses.

My throat was so tight, I could barely swallow. My heart fluttered as if I had a flock of birds in my chest.

Were we walking into a trap?

Could we really be brave enough to stare down The Menace?

A group of Horrors were huddled near a line of tall trees. They stopped talking and turned to watch us as we passed.

"I thought the HorrorLand Horrors were on *our* side," Matt said to Cranium. "I thought Ned ordered them to protect us. What are they doing here in Panic Park?"

"These Horrors work for Byron," Cranium replied. "He brought them here."

"Dangerous fellas," Maniac added. "They're not human. They'll do anything. Like ME! Hahaha!"

No one else laughed.

We stepped into the shadow of the tall mansion. Crows cawed, circling the tower roofs. Four shadow people stood stiff and alert at the top of the front stairs. Guards.

"Follow us," Cranium said. "There's a door at the side. It isn't guarded. You can sneak in there. The Menace's study is just down the hall."

My bracelet began to tingle. The heat burned my wrist.

I knew my Fear Level had to be up near the top of the meter. Did everyone else feel as afraid as I did?

If so, we were doomed to fail.

How could we show The Menace that we weren't afraid of him if we were all shaking like leaves?

We pressed ourselves close to the stone wall and crept to the side entrance. A black door hidden by a low arch. The door had no handle or knob.

"How do we open it?" Carly Beth whispered.

"Maybe I can use my key card," Matt said. He reached into his jeans pocket. He searched all his pockets. "Oh, wow," he muttered. "It's gone. I must have left it in that elevator."

"No problem," Cranium answered. "I have some useful brain powers."

He stared hard at the door and concentrated.

After a few seconds, the door slowly swung open.

"Quickly, quickly!" Cranium motioned us inside.

"Are you coming with us?" I whispered.

"We can't," Cranium replied. "If he sees us, he'll know something is up. You're on your own."

"Don't blow it!" Maniac cried.

"Remember — no fear," Cranium whispered. "Stare him down. Make the Fear Meter sink lower and lower."

We made our way into the house. I gazed around. We stood in a long, dark hallway. The walls were solid black. The ceiling was low.

I saw narrow doorways along the hall. The doors were all closed.

We began to walk. The carpet beneath our shoes was thick. We moved silently.

Matt led the way. His hands were balled into tight fists at his sides.

Michael walked behind him, his eyes narrowed, his whole body tense. On the back of his head, his monster face drooled down his shirt.

Abby and Julie walked together, hugging themselves to stop their trembling. The two shadows, Carly Beth and Billy, floated behind them.

The rest of us followed, moving silently, our eyes alert, hearts pounding.

We turned a corner. The next hall was also empty. Large black-and-white portraits lined the walls. Portraits of The Menace. Dozens of them.

Their eyes seemed to follow us as we crept silently past.

Matt raised a hand, signaling us to stop. I saw an open door at the corner. The first open door. The lights on. Someone behind the door . . .

We pushed a little closer.

I sucked in my breath when I realized we were staring at The Menace.

Luke grabbed my arm. Everyone froze. My bracelet burned a ring of pain into my wrist.

The Menace sat behind a big black desk. His study!

He leaned over an open book. His black hair fell over his forehead as he read.

I forced myself to breathe. My legs were trembling.

How could I be brave?

How could *any* of us be brave in the face of so much evil?

Matt waved us forward. We shuffled slowly toward the study door.

This was it, I knew. This was the moment. Our last chance.

Would we fail? Would we *survive*?

Moving together, we stepped up to the doorway.

And Byron burst out of the study, into the doorway. He stretched his arms straight out to block our way.

"Sorry, guys," he said. "Visiting hours are on Tuesdays!"

28

Matt shoved Byron hard in the chest. Michael head-butted him.

Byron staggered back.

We pushed our way into the study. And gathered in front of The Menace's desk.

Tall bookshelves were lined up behind him. A Fear Meter stood in the corner. The red line bobbed at 95.

"No fear!" I cried. The words burst from my mouth.

But I was shaking so hard, I couldn't think straight.

Abby and Julie picked up the chant. "No fear!" they said. And everyone repeated it.

The Menace raised his head slowly from his book. His dark eyes moved down the line, stopping for a few seconds on each one of us.

We all stared back. We didn't blink. We locked our eyes on him.

"No fear! No fear! No fear!"

Luke grabbed my hand. I grabbed Sheena's hand. We all held hands and kept up the chant.

"No fear! No fear!"

As we chanted, I could feel my fear slipping away. I felt stronger. I felt it working.

"No fear! No fear! No fear!"

We can do this! I thought.

We can stare him down. We can defeat him!

The red line on the Fear Meter hadn't moved. It stayed at 95.

The Menace slowly closed the book. He clasped his hands on top of his desk. He stared back at us for a while.

His face was a blank. No expression at all. His dark eyes didn't reveal a thing.

"No fear! No fear!"

And then . . . The Menace slapped his hands down on the desktop. He tossed back his head and laughed.

"How STUPID can you be?" he shouted.

We cut off our chant. Luke and Sheena let go of my hands.

The Menace jumped to his feet. His desk chair clattered back against the bookshelves behind him. "Do you really think a *staring contest* can defeat ME?" he boomed.

"Or ME?" his second face cried.

The red line on the Fear Meter jumped to 97.

The Menace leaned over his desk, and I saw a computer keyboard in front of him. He tapped a few keys.

"Let's see . . . Let's see what we can do," he muttered to himself.

I heard a loud hum. The whole room started to vibrate.

The Menace tapped more keys on his keyboard. "Let's see . . ." A cold smile spread over his face.

"You evil thing!" his red face cried. "You wouldn't do that to them — *would* you?"

The Menace nodded. He tapped more keys. "No fear?" he said. "Is that your slogan? Well . . . my slogan is MORE FEAR!"

The room vibrated harder. I could feel the floor move beneath my shoes.

My ear itched. I felt strange. Suddenly, I couldn't hear well.

I reached up to scratch my ear . . . and felt something warm and wet inside it. . . .

"Oh, nooo!" A moan escaped my throat as I pulled something from my ear.

A worm!

A fat brown worm.

I held it up in front of me. I could hear kids screaming all around me. But I could only think about the worm, alive, wriggling between my fingers.

And then I gagged — and reached into my mouth. And pulled another fat, sticky worm from under my tongue.

I turned and saw Boone pulling worms from his nose. Worms dangled from both his nostrils.

I saw worms crawling in Sabrina's hair. She started to tug at them, screaming and pulling them from her scalp.

Beside me, Sheena pulled a long worm from her mouth. It seemed to stretch as she pulled it. She kept spitting . . . spitting . . . and another worm poked out from between her lips.

Kids cried and screamed for help. We struggled and squirmed and choked, pulling worm after worm from our mouths, our ears, our noses.

"Go ahead!" The Menace exclaimed. "Why aren't you staring at me *now*? Go ahead! See how it works out for you!"

"Oh, nooooo!" I let out a sharp cry when I saw the Fear Meter.

At the top! The red line had climbed to 99!

"We never should have listened to those villains!" Matt screamed. "We've been TRICKED! It's a TRAP! A horrible TRAP!"

29

I pulled a worm from my hair and tossed it to the floor. Worms slithered around our shoes. Sabrina pulled one from her nose.

I kept licking my lips. I couldn't get the worm taste from my mouth.

My brain leaped crazily from thought to thought. We had to do *something*. We were as good as dead.

And suddenly, a joke popped into my head. A joke Luke had told me.

I turned to him. "What's worse than finding a worm in your apple?" I asked. "Finding *half* a worm!"

He stared at me. Then he giggled.

I gasped. Did the room shake? Did I really see everything shrink a little?

"Luke — keep laughing!" I said.

I glanced at the Fear Meter. The red line had dropped to 98.

"Lizzy," Luke said, "what's the last thing that goes through a bug's mind when it hits a windshield?"

I shrugged.

"The rest of its body!" Luke said.

We both laughed.

Again, I felt the room jolt. This time, I was sure. I really did see everything in it shrink.

Sheena and Sabrina laughed. "Tell that one to the others," Sabrina said.

Luke repeated his joke. Everyone laughed.

The red line on the Fear Meter sank to 90.

"STOP!" The Menace screamed. "Stop it! You're making us shrink!"

We kept laughing.

I kicked worms off my shoes, tossed back my head, and laughed.

"What do you get when you cut a worm in two?" Luke shouted. "The Menace!"

It didn't make much sense. But we all laughed anyway. We laughed and laughed.

"Stop it! STOP it — right now!" Both of The Menace's faces were screaming now. "I'm warning you! We're shrinking! Growing tinier . . ."

Our laughter washed away our fear. And as our fear faded, the red line on the meter sank lower and lower. 80 . . . 70 . . .

"Stop it!" The Menace screeched again. "Can't you see? Can't you see what's happening?"

And then his words sent a chill of horror over the room — and silenced us all.

"Don't you fools realize what you are doing? Don't you see that if Panic Park shrinks away, you'll be nowhere? If Panic Park disappears, *you* disappear with it!"

30

"He's LYING!" Michael shouted. "He knows we're beating him, and so he's lying!"

"Keep laughing, guys!" Sheena cried. "Let's shrink him away! Let's watch that meter drop!"

"No — wait!" Boone said. "Maybe he's telling the truth. If Panic Park vanishes, where will we *be*?"

"Maybe we just vanish, too," I said.

"We'll never get home," Sabrina murmured.

"That means he's telling the truth," I said. "Yes. Everything looks the same. That means we're shrinking along with everything else!"

And as he said those words, the red line on the Fear Meter jumped back to 80.

"That's more like it!" The Menace cried.

"Way to go, guys!" his red face exclaimed. "Be afraid! Be very afraid!"

Matt turned to the rest of us. His dark eyes were wild with fear. "What choice do we have? If we defeat The Menace . . . if we make him and his park shrink and disappear . . . maybe we disappear, too!"

"But we're also dead meat if we make the meter go all the way up," Carly Beth said.

The Menace grinned. "Go ahead! Talk about it! Talk about how scared you are! I love it! LOVE it!"

We stared at him. Both of his faces were grinning now, urging us on.

The red line on the Fear Meter was quickly sliding back to the top.

And then I heard Byron shout behind us. I turned to see him scuffling with Dr. Maniac.

The two wrestled for a moment. And then Maniac swung his cape around Byron. He twisted it around and around the struggling Horror. Then he unfurled it fast — and sent Byron spinning out of the room.

Slappy, Inspector Cranium with Dr. Crawler wrapped around his arm, the staggering mummy, and Captain Ben marched into the room behind Dr. Maniac. The ugly mask floated in the doorway, its lips bobbing silently up and down.

"What is the *meaning* of this?" The Menace shouted angrily. "When I want you freaks, I'll rattle your cages!"

Slappy stepped up to the desk. He stared at The Menace. His painted lips were locked in an evil grin.

"Who ever said two heads are better than

one?" he cried. "You're an insult to the word UGLY!"

The other villains laughed.

The room shook. I could *feel* it shrink.

"When you were born, the doctor slapped the wrong end!" Slappy told The Menace.

That made us all laugh.

The red line sank to 50 on the meter.

Slappy leaned toward The Menace. "When your mother asked your father to take out the garbage, she meant YOU!"

More laughter.

"Is that your face — or did your neck puke up your breakfast this morning?"

"Keep laughing! Keep laughing, everyone!" Cranium shouted. He turned to The Menace and shook a fist in the air. "We're not afraid of you anymore!"

The Menace shook his fists back and let out an angry squeal. His voice was tiny now. He was growing smaller.

"Stop it! Stop it! Are you CRAZY?" he whined in his little voice.

I gasped as his second face started to change. Its eyes closed. Its mouth drooped. It let out a long, low moan.

And as I stared in shock, the red color faded to gray . . . the nose melted . . . melted like candle wax . . . dripped over the sagging, melting lips.

"Look! Look at that!" I cried, pointing.

126

We all gasped in shock as The Menace's second face melted away. It folded over itself — like cake batter pouring out of a bowl — and dripped slowly down the back of The Menace's black jacket.

"Are you crazy? Are you *crazy*?" The Menace repeated in his tiny voice. "Look what you've done! He was my *only friend*! You'll pay! You'll all pay!"

Slappy raised his face to the ceiling and cackled. Dr. Crawler hissed and snapped his powerful jaws. The villains were cheering and celebrating.

The red line on the Fear Meter had dropped out of sight.

But I couldn't be happy about it. A jolt of fear tightened my throat.

"Stop!" I cried. "The Menace is shrinking. The room is shrinking. But what will happen to us? If everything disappears . . ."

"Are we ALL going to disappear?" Matt cried.

The room grew silent.

Dr. Maniac's mouth dropped open. "Uh-oh," he murmured.

"This was all YOUR idea!" Slappy rasped at Maniac.

Maniac shook his head. "My bad. My bad. We might be in a little trouble here, guys. Does anyone have a Plan B?"

Cranium turned to the door. "We've got to hurry," he said.

"It's all ssshhhrinking," Dr. Crawler hissed. "I can feel it. The Menace's whole world . . . it's ssshhhhrinking away."

"We've got to run — before it's too late!" Slappy rasped.

"Do you really think you can defeat Karloff Mennis? Do you really think you can beat The Menace?" The Menace pounded his little desk with his black-gloved hands.

"I know the way out. Follow me!" Cranium ordered. "Maybe we can make it in time!"

We all turned and stampeded from the office.

The Menace's cries rang after us as we thundered down the long hall.

"Where are we going?" Luke asked, trotting beside me. "What makes you think these guys know where they're going?"

"Do we have a choice?" I replied.

My poor brother couldn't hide his fear. But we were *all* scared.

How much time did we have before Panic Park totally disappeared?

RIDE THE WHIRLWIND.

I read the sign above the entrance to the low white building as we ran up to it.

"Here we are," Dr. Maniac called, pointing to the sign. "Everybody in!"

"Wait a minute!" Matt grabbed his arm. "What are you trying to do to us?"

"Yeah," Michael said. "The Menace told us about The Whirlwind. He said it scrambles your brain. He said it turns your brain to mush."

"The Menace was lying," Slappy rasped. "He was trying to frighten you away from this building."

"We've all used The Whirlwind to go back and forth to HorrorLand," Cranium said. "Britney and Molly used it once. It's faster than the mirrors."

I turned to Britney. "Is he telling the truth? Is *this* the building you used to return to HorrorLand?"

Britney scrunched up her face. "Maybe ..." she replied. "I ... I remember it was very windy."

We pushed up to the entrance. I could hear a ferocious wind inside, thundering against the walls, whistling as it blew.

A chill ran down my back. Would it be like stepping into a *hurricane*?

I heard a shout behind us. I turned and saw The Menace and Byron running across the park toward us. A big group of shadow people followed close behind them.

"Don't look back at them!" Slappy ordered. "Quick, you dummies! Open the door. Jump into The Whirlwind — and we're all OUTTA here!"

But I couldn't turn away from the The Menace and the others, running closer . . . closer . . . As the whole park shrank away. The rides, the food carts, the buildings, the trees — everything — growing smaller . . . smaller . . . About to vanish, as it should have forty years ago!

Matt grabbed the entrance door handle. "It . . . it's padlocked!" he shouted. "It's locked tight!"

I glanced back — and gasped. I saw Jillian and Jackson! The two traitors. The Menace's spies.

They were speeding toward us, far in front of the others. And I could see the hard glares on their faces.

"They're coming to stop us!" I cried. "They're coming to keep us out of The Whirlwind!"

"Hurry!" Slappy screamed at Matt.

Matt tugged hard on the padlock. He pulled it, jerking it with all his strength.

"It . . . won't budge!" he cried. "We're locked out!"

Jillian and Jackson stormed up to the entrance.

"Get away!" Carly Beth screamed. "Look at me! I'm a shadow! Look at all of us! Haven't we suffered enough because of you?"

I glanced back. Panic Park was tiny now. Like a world inside a snow globe.

The Menace and Byron looked like little mice scrambling toward us.

"You've got to believe us!" Jillian cried. "Jackson and I — we didn't know our powers came from The Menace! We didn't know he was controlling us!"

"Cranium put headphones over our ears. He said it was a brain test!" Jackson cried. "But that's when The Menace took control of us!"

"We didn't want to work for him!" Jillian added. "He forced us. But now he can't control us. His power has shrunk with him!"

"I'll prove we're on your side!" Jackson said. "I can open the door."

"I'll help you!" Cranium cried, bumping up next to Jackson.

The two of them concentrated on the padlock. Concentrated . . .

And the lock *snapped* off!

I screamed as the door flew open. A ferocious blast of cold wind slammed the door against the front wall.

Blast after blast roared out of the building.

I saw Matt shouting something to the rest of us. But I couldn't hear him over the thunderous wind.

Matt lowered his head — and dove into the wind.

I couldn't breathe. The cold wind slammed into me, like an ocean wave. I toppled onto my back. Luke pulled me to my feet.

We screamed as the wind lifted both of us off the ground. Another blast swirled around us — and *pulled* us to the building.

As I sailed into the swirling gusts, I glanced back. One last look at Panic Park.

It was so tiny now . . . nothing left . . . just a shiny bubble floating against the colorless sky.

And then the bubble POPPED.

I spun away — and hurtled into The Whirlwind.

A powerful gust swept under me and lifted me . . . carried me over the floor.

Like flying, I thought. *Flying out of control.*

Flying WHERE?

I soared high in a long blue tunnel, then floated lower.

I could see the other kids ahead of me. And then a tidal wave of wind swept me around, and the kids were behind me.

I pressed my hands over my ears, struggling to shut out the roar. I closed my eyes and let the wind carry me . . . carry me through the long blue tunnel.

And then I felt a hard tug, and I began to spin. Harder . . . harder . . . whirling as if I were in the center of a raging cyclone.

And then the wind stopped.

Silence. A sudden, horrifying silence.

The wind stopped and let go of me —

— and I started to drop.

Straight down. Down . . .

I screamed all the way.

I landed gently on my feet.

Warm air brushed my face. Dizzy. My body swayed. So hard to stand.

The fierce wind was gone, but I could still feel it tingling my skin.

I took a deep breath and held it. And gazed around. "Luke? Are you okay?"

"I . . . I guess." My brother stood right next to me, shaking off the chill of the swirling winds. "Where are we?"

I spun around. And saw Carly Beth. Not a shadow.

She and Billy were staring at each other, their faces shocked at first, and then grinning with relief.

"We're back! We're not shadows!"

Robby held his hands in front of his face. "I can see myself! I'm not invisible! Yaaaay!"

And we all cheered when we saw Britney with

her normal head. Abby and Julie had stopped shaking. And Michael was back to having only one face.

"We're back! We're back to normal!"

And we started to celebrate even before we realized we were standing in a parking lot. I saw the green-and-purple entrance sign, rows and rows away from us.

"It's HorrorLand!" I shouted, pumping my fists in the air.

Yes. We were standing in the HorrorLand parking lot. And before we could celebrate for long, there were our parents.

Everyone's parents. Moving down the row of cars toward us.

Dad studied his watch. "You're late," he said. "Where have you all been?"

"Where have YOU been all this time?" I blurted out.

Mom wrinkled up her forehead. "Didn't they tell you, Lizzy? They took all of us adults to our own hotel. We had a great time. We made so many new friends."

Dad frowned. "But we've been waiting for you kids here. Time to go home."

I glanced around at the other family reunions. Lots of hugs and happy greetings.

I whispered to Luke. "None of them have any idea of the danger we were in. Look at them all, grinning and laughing. Clueless."

"Let's keep them that way!" Luke said. "How could we ever explain it?"

A green-and-purple Horror watched from the side. He had a smile on his face.

I walked over to him. "You're Ned, aren't you?" I asked.

His smile grew wider. "Monster X to *you!*" he said.

"Thank you," I said. "I think we *all* want to thank you!"

"Come on, you two!" Dad called. "We have a long drive ahead of us." He gave us a push toward the car.

"Lizzy, look at your hair," Mom said, brushing it down with her hand. "It's all wild and crazy. Why is it such a mess?"

"Uh . . . I went on a very fast ride," I said.

That night, how happy was I to be back in my own bedroom?

Three guesses.

But as I started to unpack, I couldn't get Panic Park out of my mind.

I thought about the little shadow girl, pleading with me in that faraway voice: *Find me . . . Can you find me?*

I pictured that black-and-white world . . . the dark, empty buildings . . . the rides and shops and restaurants, all closed, all shades of gray. Shades from another world.

And again, I saw the park shrinking away . . . growing smaller and smaller. So tiny — and then gone.

A whole park. A whole *world*. Gone with a tiny *pop*.

I yawned. I was so tired, I could barely keep my eyes open.

I pulled out pairs of jeans from the suitcase. They were still folded. I never had a chance to wear them.

And what was this? My hand felt something hard. And big.

Something taking up all the room in the suitcase.

I pushed aside some T-shirts and gasped. "Oh, noooo."

I lifted it out of the case. A ventriloquist dummy.

I rubbed its painted hair. It had an ugly grin on its wooden lips.

"How did *this* thing get in my suitcase?" I murmured.

And then I let out a cry as the dummy's eyes slowly opened. And its ugly grin grew wider.

"Well, well," it rasped in a tinny voice. "Lookin' good, Lizzy."

It blinked its eyes and gazed up at me. "Ready to start a whole new story? This one will *really* give you goosebumps! Hahahahaha!"

THE END

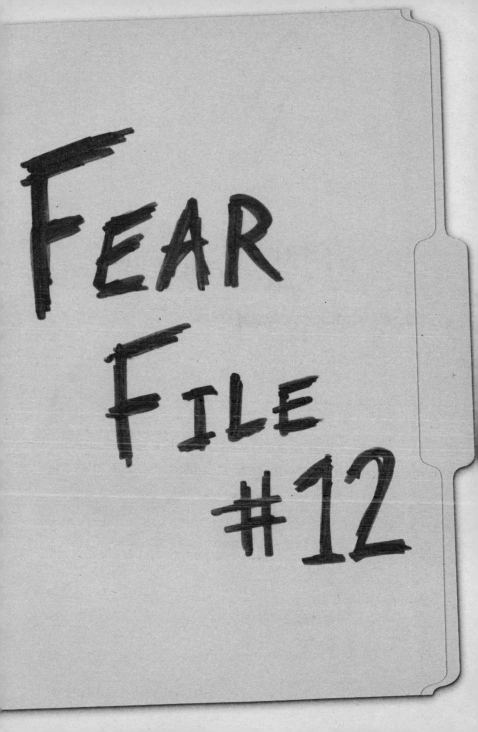

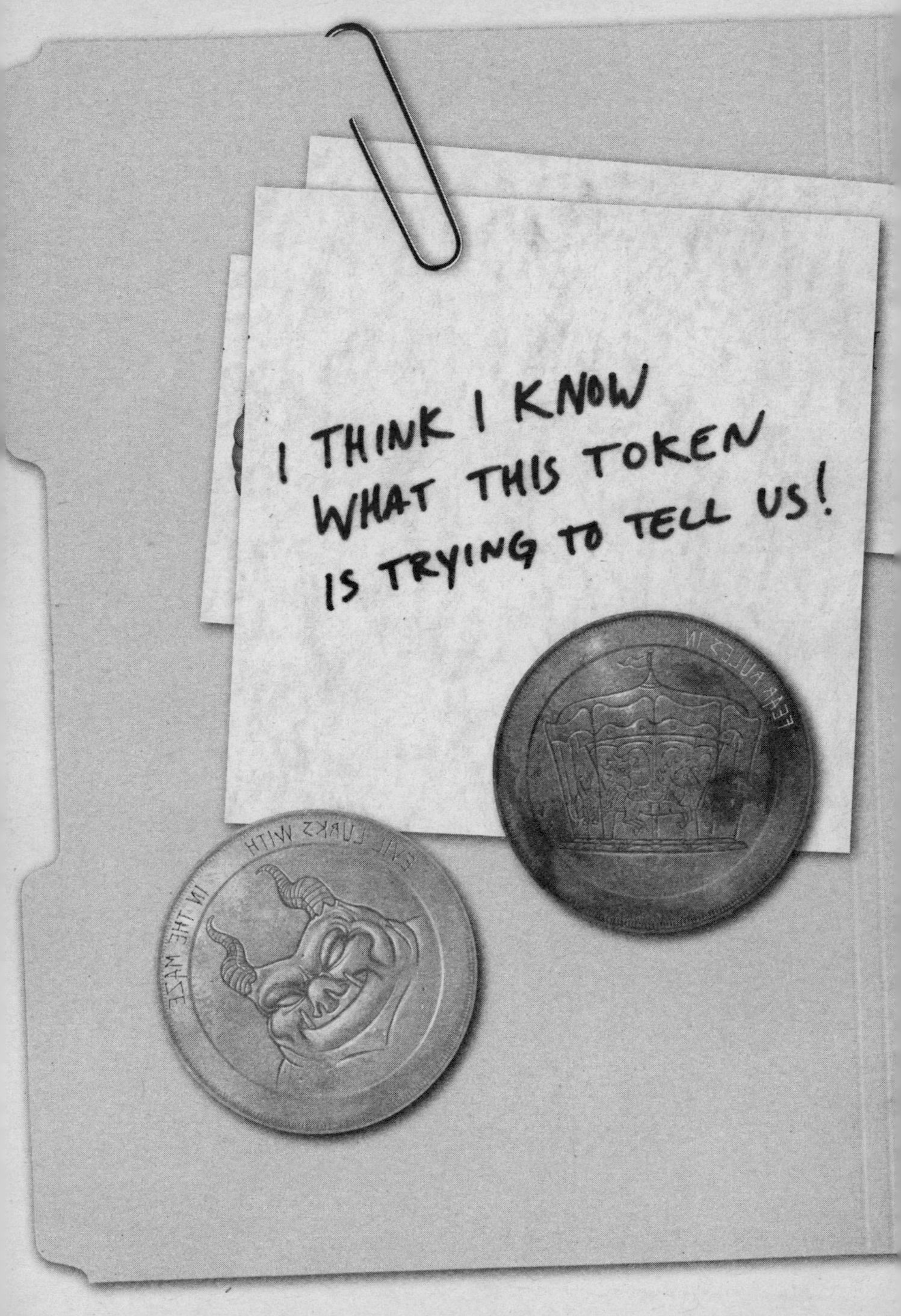
I THINK I KNOW
WHAT THIS TOKEN
IS TRYING TO TELL US!

Dear Very Special Guest,

From time to time we conduct guest surveys to see how you are enjoying your stay and what you are learning about our amusement park.

Please complete the following survey and leave it at The Crocodile Café. You will receive a complimentary token.

Horrors hate to be pinched.   ❏ True   ❏ False

Snakes are a Horror's best friend.   ❏ True   ❏ False

The Ferris Wheel is the Scariest Ride
in HorrorLand.   ❏ True   ❏ False

Dr. Maniac was raised in Werewolf Village.   ❏ True   ❏ False

Byron's code name is The Keeper.   ❏ True   ❏ False

There is no 13th floor in Stagger Inn.   ❏ True   ❏ False

*IT'S A TRAP —
THEY WANT TO SEE
HOW MUCH WE KNOW!*

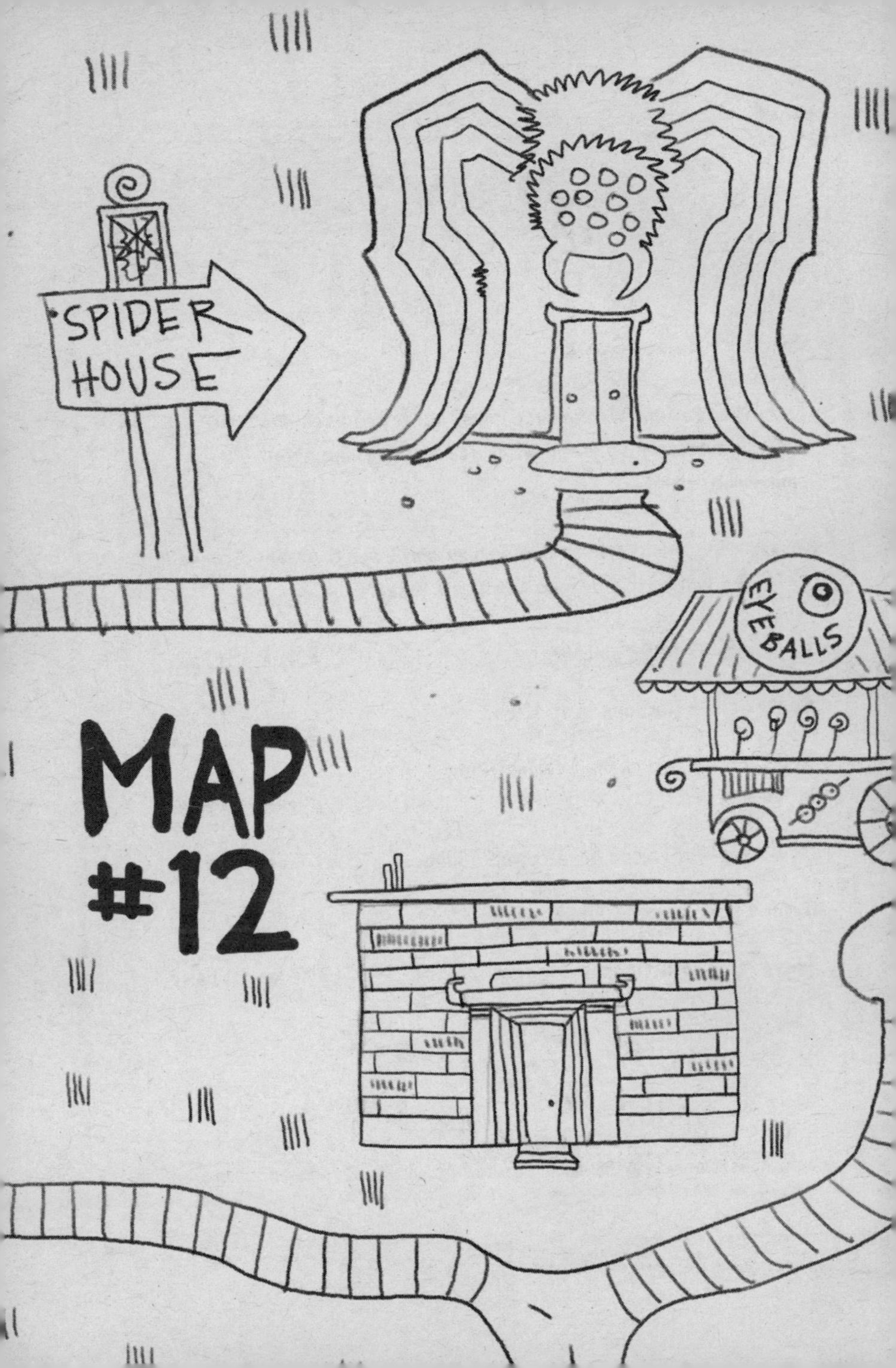
SPIDER HOUSE
EYEBALLS
MAP #12

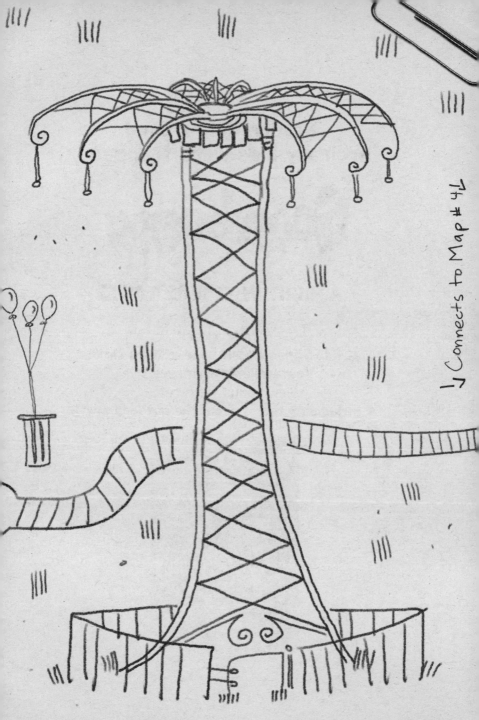

Connects to Map #4

Before HorrorLand,
ordinary kids were trapped in

A NIGHT IN TERROR TOWER

Take a peek
at R.L. Stine's classic bone-chilling thriller.
Now available with exclusive
new bonus features —
including a secret from the author's past!

1

"I'm scared, Eddie said.

I shivered and zipped my coat up to my chin. "Eddie, this was *your* idea," I told my brother. "I didn't beg and plead to see the Terror Tower. You did."

He raised his brown eyes to the tower. A strong gust of wind fluttered his dark brown hair. "I have a strange feeling about it, Sue. A bad feeling."

I made a disgusted face. "Eddie, you are such a wimp! You have a bad feeling about going to the movies!"

"Only *scary* movies," he mumbled.

"You're ten years old," I said sharply. "It's time to stop being scared of your own shadow. It's just an old castle with a tower," I said, gesturing toward it. "Hundreds of tourists come here every day."

"But they used to torture people here," Eddie said, suddenly looking very pale. "They used to lock people in the Tower and let them starve to death."

"Hundreds of years ago," I told him. "They don't torture people here anymore, Eddie. Now they just sell postcards."

We both gazed up at the gloomy old castle built of gray stones, darkened over time. Its narrow towers rose up like two stiff arms at its sides.

Storm clouds hovered low over the dark towers. The bent old trees in the courtyard shivered in the wind. It didn't feel like spring. The air was heavy and cold. I felt a raindrop on my forehead. Then another on my cheek.

A perfect London day, I thought. *A perfect day to visit the famous Terror Tower.*

This was our first day in England, and Eddie and I had been sightseeing all over London. Our parents had to be at a conference at our hotel. So they signed us up with a tour group, and off we went.

We toured the British Museum, walked through Harrods department store, visited Westminster Abbey and Trafalgar Square.

For lunch, we had bangers and mash (sausages and mashed potatoes) at a real English pub. Then the tour group took a great bus ride, sitting on top of a bright red double-decker bus.

London was just as I had imagined it. Big and crowded. Narrow streets lined with little shops and jammed with those old-fashioned–looking black taxis. The sidewalks were filled with people from all over the world.

Of course my scaredy-cat brother was totally nervous about traveling around a strange city on our own. But I'm twelve and a lot less wimpy than he is. And I managed to keep him pretty calm.

I was totally surprised when Eddie begged to visit the Terror Tower.

Mr. Starkes, our bald, red-faced tour guide, gathered the group together on the sidewalk. There were about twelve of us, mostly old people. Eddie and I were the only kids.

Mr. Starkes gave us a choice. Another museum — or the Tower.

"The Tower! The Tower!" Eddie pleaded. "I've *got* to see the Terror Tower!"

We took a long bus ride to the outskirts of the city. The shops gave way to rows of tiny redbrick houses. Then we passed even older houses, hidden behind stooped trees and low, ivy-covered walls.

When the bus pulled to a stop, we climbed out and followed a narrow street made of bricks, worn smooth over the centuries. The street ended at a high wall. Behind the wall, the Terror Tower rose up darkly.

"Hurry, Sue!" Eddie tugged my sleeve. "We'll lose the group!"

"They'll wait for us," I told my brother. "Stop worrying, Eddie. We won't get lost."

We jogged over the old bricks and caught up

with the others. Wrapping his long black over-
coat around him, Mr. Starkes led the way through
the entrance.

He stopped and pointed at a pile of gray stones
in the large grass-covered courtyard. "That wall
was the original castle wall," he explained. "It was
built by the Romans in about the year 400.
London was a Roman city then."

Only a small section of the wall still stood. The
rest had crumbled or fallen. I couldn't believe I
was staring at a wall that was over fifteen hundred
years old!

We followed Mr. Starkes along the path that
led to the castle and its towers. "This was built
by the Romans to be a walled fort," the tour
guide told us. "After the Romans left, it became
a prison. That started many years of cruelty and
torture within these walls."

I pulled my little camera from my coat pocket
and took a picture of the Roman wall. Then I
turned and snapped a few pictures of the castle.
The sky had darkened even more. I hoped the
pictures would come out.

"This was London's first debtor prison," Mr.
Starkes explained as he led the way. "If you were
too poor to pay your bills, you were sent to prison.
Which meant that you could *never* pay your bills!
So you stayed in prison forever."

We passed a small guardhouse. It was about
the size of a phone booth, made of white stones,

with a slanted roof. I thought it was empty. But to my surprise, a gray-uniformed guard stepped out of it, a rifle perched stiffly on his shoulder.

I turned back and gazed at the dark wall that surrounded the castle grounds. "Look, Eddie," I whispered. "You can't see any of the city outside the wall. It's as if we really stepped back in time."

He shivered. I don't know if it was because of my words or because of the sharp wind that blew through the old courtyard.

The castle cast a deep shadow over the path. Mr. Starkes led us up to a narrow entrance at the side. Then he stopped and turned back to the group.

I was startled by the tense, sorrowful expression on his face. "I am so sorry to give you this bad news," he said, his eyes moving slowly from one of us to the next.

"Huh? Bad news?" Eddie whispered, moving closer to me.

"You will all be imprisoned in the north tower," Mr. Starkes announced sternly. "There you will be tortured until you tell us the real reason why you chose to come here."

PLACE ON EARTH!

THIS BOOK IS YOUR TICKET TO

www.EnterHorrorLand.com

CHECKLIST #12

- [ ] I scream, you scream, we all scream for...FROZEN EYEBALLS? Take time for a tasty treat...HorrorLand style.

- [ ] Uh-oh, black balloons on the loose. This can't be good.

- [ ] Step right up to the Free-Fall Bungee Jump: Hope you're not afraid of heights!

- [ ] QUESTION: What's teeming with tarantulas and swarming with spiders? ANSWER: You are, unless you can fight your way out of this dangerous web.

- [ ] Mirror, mirror, on the wall, who's the SCARIEST of them all?

UNLOCK THE 12TH MAP!

_____
USER NAME

_____
PASSWORD

For more frights, check out the Goosebumps HorrorLand video game!